VACANCY

VACANCY

K. R. Alexander

Scholastic Inc.

Copyright © 2021 by Alex R. Kahler writing as K. R. Alexander

All rights reserved. Published by Scholastic Inc., *Publishers since 1920*. SCHOLASTIC and associated logos are trademarks and/or registered trademarks of Scholastic Inc.

The publisher does not have any control over and does not assume any responsibility for author or third-party websites or their content.

No part of this publication may be reproduced, stored in a retrieval system, or transmitted in any form or by any means, electronic, mechanical, photocopying, recording, or otherwise, without written permission of the publisher. For information regarding permission, write to Scholastic Inc., Attention: Permissions Department, 557 Broadway, New York, NY 10012.

ISBN 978-1-338-70215-6

10 9 8 7 6 5 4 3   21 22 23 24 25

Printed in the U.S.A.   40
First printing 2021

Book design by Baily Crawford

For those who understand
that to dream we must
first enter the dark

I'll never forget the first time I saw the Carlisle Hotel in person.

After my mom died, my dad wanted a fresh start. He kept saying he wanted to get out of the city and reconnect. With nature. With the place he and Mom had met. With me, if he could. We'd grown so distant since Mom died. I knew he wanted to reconnect with me most of all.

He talked about the town all the time: Gold River. He talked about it so much that even though I'd never been there, I felt like I'd lived there my whole life.

I listened to his stories. I felt the pull, too. Gold River was home—it was where I was meant to be.

Which is how I ended up halfway across the country in the tiny tourist trap of a town at the base of Crossback Mountain, one of the biggest, oldest ski resorts in the area.

Gold River was sprawling but quaint at the same time, perfectly made to invite in eager skiers. There were some ski-repair shops whose names I knew from the multiple applications my dad had sent in. There were cute diners and high-end restaurants to warm up in after a day on the slopes. And if tourists wanted to rent a chalet with Swiss lattice and a steep roof, there were a few dozen to choose from. There was only one place they couldn't stay—

The Carlisle Hotel.

The Carlisle was perched at the edge of town, surrounded by pine trees and backing up to some abandoned ski runs. Huge and ancient, the size of a city block, with wood-shuttered windows and gilded front doors—the type of hotel millionaires once flocked to in droves. The type of hotel that once promised luxurious furnishings and elegant dinners and dramatic views from every firelit room.

But not anymore.

I felt my breath catch the first time I passed it. It was beautiful, but also sad and empty.

That's exactly how I felt then—sad and empty.

I had felt that way for what seemed like forever.

I stayed away from the hotel at first. Moving in August meant I could start school like everyone else. I made friends and learned my way around the town before the holiday season kicked in. In those first few weeks, the hotel wasn't the only building that felt abandoned. Only for the Carlisle, the emptiness wasn't seasonal.

Eventually the mountains got their first dusting of snow, and all the tourists flocked back, eager to get back on the slopes. The chalets filled. The shops bustled.

The Carlisle stayed vacant.

It had been that way for almost thirty-three years.

I should be honest, though: That wasn't the first time I truly saw the hotel.

I first saw the Carlisle in my dreams.

Three years ago, on the night of my tenth birthday.

Before my mom died. Before the move to Gold River.

I dreamed of walking up that hedge-lined drive leading to the front doors.

I dreamed of wandering inside. Through the lobby with its massive staircase, crimson carpets, golden chandeliers, and marble reception desks. Past the indoor pool and spa that smelled of chlorine and eucalyptus. Past the meeting rooms and dining halls filled with ancient statues, Renaissance paintings, and round tables with crisp white linens and glittering crystal.

Down a long, dark hall.

A hall so unlike everything else in the Carlisle.

Dark.

Narrow.

Flickering.

Forgotten.

I remember the tug that led me forward.

My destination?

A plain
  white
  door

at the end of a plain
white
hall.

I remember what happened when I reached the door.

I remember, because I've had that dream or some form of it every night since.

I always get to the door,
but I
never
get
past
it.

I touch my hand to the old doorknob.
I start to turn it.
I am filled by fear.
And then I wake up.
But I know what waits behind the door.
I know it in the darkest corner of my being.
Death.
All that waits in the Carlisle is death.

1

"You know what Saturday is, don't you?" Rohan asks.

My stomach twists with fear and excitement.

"Of course we know," Mira says. Despite the crowded lunchroom, her voice is soft. She looks down at her tray while she says it, her dark cheeks flushing in embarrassment. "You haven't stopped talking about it all month."

Rohan grins at her discomfort. Mira's right—Rohan hasn't dropped the subject since the end of November. Now, a few days before winter break, it's practically all he can talk about.

"And I'm not going to stop talking about it now,"

he says. He pushes his glasses back up the bridge of his nose, his brown eyes gleaming with excitement. "This is our one chance to *finally* be among the cool kids. *No one* has ever completed the Dare. All we have to do is spend one full night in the Carlisle Hotel. That's it. If we do it, we'd be the most popular kids in Gold River, like, ever."

Mira sighs. This is the same thing he's said every day since the word spread that the seventh-grade Dare would take place this Saturday at ten. Everyone who wanted to be anyone was expected to show up and test their bravery.

"I don't know," Mira mutters.

Rohan turns to me.

"What about you, Jasmine?" he asks. "Can I count you in?"

I look to Mira. She and I have spent countless nights talking about the Dare. The truth is, I don't really mind the idea of staying overnight in the Carlisle Hotel; if I'm honest, I want to know why I've always felt drawn there. But Mira is scared to death of it. Unlike me, she grew up here, which means she's grown up with all the scary stories associated with the hotel. Rumors that it never reopened because a bunch of people had mysteriously died there. Or that it's haunted. Or cursed. That it still craves human souls and will snatch up anyone brave—or stupid—enough to step foot there.

That's the whole point of the Dare: Around here, kids believe that if you stay a full night, you'll never be allowed to leave.

Despite my dreams drawing me in, I'm still not sure. It could be dangerous. Mira, though, is pretty convinced—she most definitely does *not* want to go in. Ever. There's no way to answer without upsetting either of my new friends, which is the last thing I want to do.

"I'll go if Mira goes," I reply.

I hope it's the right thing to say, but it's clear from the glare she shoots me that it isn't.

Rohan whoops with glee.

"See! You can't chicken out now, Mira. If the *new girl* is willing to do it, you have to as well."

She doesn't look at either of us, just stares at her tray of food.

A second later, she flinches as something smacks the back of her head.

I look over to see a fry drop to the floor.

She grumbles, but she ignores it. She always ignores it. And yet, kids still pick on her, maybe because she tries so hard to pretend the bullying doesn't exist.

Rohan lowers his voice and leans in.

"Come on, Mira," he says. "We need this. You know we do. If we do this, maybe they'll leave us alone. I'm not saying I believe it will make us popular, but it might make us *safe*. I don't want to keep dealing with this all through high school. You know it will only get worse."

Mira keeps staring at her tray.

"How do you know?" she asks.

"Because everyone—"

"No," she interrupts. "How do you know we'll make it the entire night?"

Rohan reaches across the table and takes her hand. "Because the three of us are a team. We can do anything," he says. He looks at me when he says it, and it makes my heart warm to know he thinks of me as a true friend, even though I've only been here a few months. I didn't have any friends like that back in Florida.

Another fry flies past us, just barely missing my ear. Behind us, a table of kids erupts into laughter.

I glance over my shoulder to see Bradley among them. Most of the kids look away when I glare at them, but not Bradley. He acts like he runs this town, and I guess in a lot of ways he does; his dad is the mayor, and he lives in a manor nearly as big as the Carlisle. This is something he points out all the time, whenever I'm in earshot. Somehow he knows I live in a tiny house on the outskirts.

Bradley isn't scared or ashamed of anything. He stares right back at me and sticks out his tongue.

My hands ball into fists. Ugh. I wish I could show him.

There *is* a way I could show him.

I look back to Mira and say, "All I want to do is wipe that smug smile off Bradley's face. I don't know why he's such a jerk to us."

Without missing a beat, Rohan points to himself. "Band geek." Then to Mira. "Mathlete." And me. "New girl." He shrugs. "We've basically got targets painted on our backs."

"It isn't right," I say. It's not that I was popular in Florida—honestly, it was the opposite. So far, Rohan and Mira are the best friends I've ever had.

But the fact that we're being picked on, let alone by someone as boring as Bradley, makes my blood boil. I thought these tourist towns were supposed to be friendly to everyone, but I guess there are mean people everywhere.

"Of course it isn't right," Rohan says. "But there's not much we can do to change it. Some kids are meant to be bullies, and some are meant to be picked on. It's like the natural order or something."

"Don't tell me you actually believe that," I say.

He shrugs again and goes back to eating his sandwich.

"Of course I don't believe it," Rohan says. "But that doesn't matter so much when people like Bradley do. The only way we're going to change things is to make him realize we aren't his victims. And we do that by proving we're braver than he is. We do it by staying overnight at the Carlisle."

Mira groans as another fry lands on her sandwich. This fry definitely had a bite taken out of it. She pushes her tray forward and stands.

"I'm not hungry anymore," she says. "I think I'm gonna go to the library until recess."

"Just promise me you'll think about it," Rohan pushes. "We can do it together. You don't have to be scared."

Mira bites her lip. "I'm not scared," she says after a moment. "I just . . . it feels wrong. Like we're playing into their game. Besides, you know it's illegal to step foot on the Carlisle property. What if we got caught?"

"It's a risk I'm willing to take," he says.

Something smacks into the back of my head. I reach back and pull a fry out of my curls. Anger burns inside me, but I don't look back to Bradley. I don't want to let him know he gets under my skin.

The words leave my lips before I can stop them, before I even realize I was going to speak them: "Me too," I say. I lock eyes with Rohan. "I'm in. But no pressure, Mira. Rohan and I can do it alone if you don't want to."

"I'll think about it," Mira says with a sigh. She picks up her tray as she stands to leave. "I just don't know if being popular is worth doing something like this."

"It will be fine," Rohan says. "It's just one night. The stories are just stories—I bet there are some high schoolers hanging out at the hotel trying to scare us off. Nothing *bad* ever happens. Kids have been doing the Dare for years, and no one's died."

Instantly, my dreams flash into my mind. Walking down the long, flickering white hallway. The imposing door at the end.

The terrible fate behind it.

Maybe Rohan is right. Maybe no one new has died staying overnight at the Carlisle.

At least, not yet.

2

I wait for Mira after school.

Even though it's literally freezing out and it's already getting dark, I stand outside next to a snow-bank. Maybe it's another reason people here think I'm weird, but I really like the winter. I mean, everyone in Gold River *likes* winter—the whole town is built around snow sports, so it's sort of a requirement. But I dunno. Maybe it's because it's the opposite of what I'm used to, but there's something about standing outside in the snow that makes me feel so *alive*. The way the cold makes my cheeks tingle and my breath come out in clouds, the way the snow dances down in tiny flakes or in big wet chunks that make my eye-lashes heavy. I'd stay out in the snow all day and night if I could.

It makes me think of my mother—she always told me stories of her own childhood living in cold places. The snow connects me to her.

It makes me feel free.

At least until I look up.

As I stare out at the softly falling snow, I catch sight of something that makes me feel the opposite of free.

The Carlisle Hotel.

It sits on the other side of the valley, past the Gold River, surrounded by forest and abandoned ski slopes. It almost looks like a castle from here, a squat, aban-doned fortress filled with darkness and shadows.

I have stared at its windows for hours.

Nothing has ever stared back.

But now—

Now—

Something is different.

One of the windows on the upper floor is illuminated.

The light flickers slightly, like a candle.

How is that even possible?

The hotel has been abandoned for decades, and no one steps foot there. At least not until the Dare night.

Even from here, a mile or so away, I feel a hook in my heart the moment I see it, even as chills race down my skin.

I blink, and I'm back in the hall. The flickering white hallway, pulled toward a door at the far end.

I hear something.

In the dreams, the hall has always been silent—ominously so—but now there's no mistaking it.

The faint yelling.

No.

The faint screaming, calling out my name.

Calling me forward . . . or telling me to get out?

Jasmine! Jasmine, hurry!

"Earth to Jasmine," comes a voice beside me.

I'm so surprised I actually jump back. My foot catches on the thick snow, and I tumble, landing with a heavy thump in a snowdrift.

"Whoa!" Mira says. She immediately reaches down and helps me struggle to standing, which is difficult with all my layers. "Are you okay? I didn't mean to scare you."

"Yeah," I say. I shake the snow off and look back to the Carlisle Hotel.

All the windows are dark now.

As they should be.

As they might have been all along.

My mind must be playing tricks on me.

"I was just distracted," I explain to Mira.

She follows my gaze. "You're thinking about it, aren't you?" she asks. "About doing the Dare."

I nod, though it's not the whole truth; I've felt the hotel's pull for so long now. It's not something I'm comfortable telling her, though. I'm lucky enough that I was able to make friends so quickly. I don't want to risk all that by having her think I'm crazy, or that I know about the hotel any more than she thinks I do.

"I guess I just don't understand why everyone makes such a big deal out of it," I say, wondering how she'll respond. "I mean, it's just a hotel, right?"

She looks uncomfortable.

"You've heard the stories," she says. It's not a

question. After all, Rohan's the one who told me all of them, usually with Mira right there.

I nod.

"Well, it's not just stories," she says. "They're real. I looked them up in the library's archives." She starts walking as she talks; Rohan took the bus home, and since Mira and I live a few blocks away from each other, we usually walk home together.

"The Carlisle Hotel used to be the whole reason people came to Gold River. At one time, it employed over half the town's population. We depended on it. And then, one year . . . one year, something terrible happened. No one really knows what took place. The newspaper articles just say that one morning, when the hotel staff came to relieve the night shift workers, they found that everyone—and I mean *everyone*—inside had died." She hesitates before continuing, and when she does, her voice is muffled. She talks into her scarf like she doesn't even want to hear what she's saying. "Well, okay. There was one survivor. They found her in the lobby rocking back and forth, and they never got her to say what happened. She disappeared the next day."

"Did she do it?" I ask. I look to the hotel again,

though it's quickly disappearing in the pine trees as we head through town.

Mira shakes her head. "She was never convicted. Because the strange thing was, it didn't look like there had been a struggle. The people had just dropped dead. The investigators thought maybe it was a gas leak or something, or maybe some mass poisoning. But then the coroner said that every single one of them had died . . . of fright."

I shudder, and not from the cold.

"How is that even possible?" I ask.

"No one knows. There were hundreds of guests and hotel staff there that night. Only one of them walked out of there alive. They shut down the hotel after that, obviously. Not that anyone would want to go there even if it stayed open. The town itself nearly fell apart. But they built a new ski slope on the other side of the valley, and that saved us." She looks over to the mountains on this side of the river. The season is in full swing there, and even from here I can see tiny flecks of skiers and boarders racing down the cleared courses.

"Anyway," she says, "that's why I don't want to go. Everyone else thinks it's fun and games. But people actually died there, and it feels wrong to turn it into a dare or a prank. It's disrespectful to those who lost their lives."

I nod. So that's why she doesn't want to go—it's not that she's scared, it's that she actually feels bad for the people who died there. *That's* what she means by this whole thing maybe not being worth it. It isn't about fear, or breaking the law. It's about respecting the dead.

It makes me respect her even more. It also makes me not want to push her. Though, the moment I think that, I remember Bradley's contented sneer, and want nothing more than to prove to him that we aren't cowards and he doesn't just get to pick on everyone because he's the mayor's son.

"If you don't want to do this, I understand," I say. "I totally get it. I don't think it's right, either. But I also don't want Bradley and the rest to keep making our lives miserable. This seems like the only way."

Because even though I find it strange, it's clear that the kids in this town put a *lot* of pressure on the Dare. I've heard so many horror stories of kids who skipped out and spent the rest of their school years— even up through high school—being bullied. I've seen it firsthand. I guess that's what happens when stories like the Carlisle start taking on a life of their own.

"I know," she replies. "I also know Rohan wants me to do it. And he's right—if we don't go, we're basically cursed to be the unpopular kids for the rest of our lives. Besides . . ."

She cuts off. She looks embarrassed.

"What?" I ask.

"Nothing. It's nothing."

"Come on," I say. "You can tell me anything." I immediately feel guilty—*I haven't told her everything. Not by a long shot.*

"Well . . . it's strange," she admits slowly. "I swear I feel a pull to the place. Ever since I was a little girl, I've felt it calling me. And I guess that's part of the reason I don't want to go. I'm scared of what I'll find there."

My heart jolts. So she feels pulled, too? I wonder if Rohan does as well.

I know I should say something, but I stop myself. It would only scare her more. After all, it sort of makes sense for her to be pulled to a place when she grew up listening to stories about it. What does it mean that I felt the pull before I even knew it was a real hotel?

What would she say if I admitted my dreams?

"Well," I say, ignoring the doubt, "my mom always told me that the only way to get over my fear was to face it. So maybe we need to face this. Together. But, you know—no pressure."

She nods. As if she's convincing herself. And now I feel torn—part of me really wants her to go to the hotel to see what it's hiding. The rest doesn't want to make her do anything she's against. Her next question makes my stomach twist.

"Where *is* your mom?" she asks.

"What?"

"Your mom. You've mentioned her a couple times, but you said you moved with just your dad. Did they get divorced or something?"

I hesitate. I've tried not to tell her too much about my past. It's the past, after all. But some things follow you everywhere you go.

"No," I admit. "She died a couple years ago."

Mira gasps. "I'm so sorry." She reaches out and squeezes my shoulder. "I didn't know."

"It's okay," I say. Even though it's not okay. Not at all. I miss her every day. I'd still do anything to get her back.

"You must miss her a lot," she says.

I nod. "She was my best friend in Florida. My only friend, really. We did everything together. I told her everything. When she passed away . . . when she passed away, it was like I lost a part of myself."

Mira nods as if she understands, even though she doesn't. She could never understand. But it feels a little better knowing that she's trying.

"Well," she says. "We're your family now, Rohan and me. I know it's not the same, but . . ."

I smile. "Thank you," I say.

I pull her in for a hug. But all I can think is how much I miss my mom, how much I wish she was here.

"I'm glad you moved here," she says.

Over Mira's shoulder, the Carlisle Hotel broods on its mountain. Watching. Waiting.

"Yeah," I reply. "Me too."

3

After school the next day, even though the rest of our class is in high spirits, Mira is more glum than ever. She's barely said a thing all day. Even at lunch, when Rohan once more brought up the Dare, she didn't respond. It makes me wonder if she's been dreaming about the Carlisle as well. It makes me wonder if she's going to back out.

And, okay, I know it's selfish, but I don't want her to back out. I want to get to the bottom of this. I want to go to the Carlisle with her and Rohan, but I don't want to push her. I want Bradley to stop making fun of me in the halls. I want to stop feeling like the new kid.

And, yes, I want to see what's behind that white door. Ever since I've arrived, the dreams have gotten stronger, the pull more intense. I can't sleep, and when I do, all I dream about is the corridor and the door, and when I wake, all I think about is the person calling my name. I have to follow. It feels like if I don't, the dreams will destroy me.

Rohan and Mira and I linger outside Mira's locker, watching everyone else get ready. It's Friday, which means classes are over for the next two weeks of winter break, and it shows. Kids are blaring music on their phones in the hall and dancing around as they get into their snow gear. Some of them exchange presents, while others loudly talk about all the presents they're planning on getting. Most discuss going skiing this weekend.

No one is talking about the Dare. No one wants to risk a teacher overhearing and putting a stop to it. I can tell, though, that that's all anyone is thinking about. There's a tension in the air I can almost taste.

I hate to say that it's actually exciting. I worried

that I'd be bored after moving here from a big city with beaches and beautiful sunsets and so many things to do. The Dare is the only thing in this town besides snow sports, and it's easy to get swept up in the forbidden excitement.

"Did you two want to hang out tonight?" Rohan asks.

"Sure," Mira says. "Jasmine?"

I nod, but I'm not really paying attention. I'm too busy wondering how many of these kids are going to show up at the hotel tomorrow night. How many will be brave enough to spend a full night there.

I wonder if we'll be among them. I hope we are.

Farther down the hallway, I see Bradley talking with some of his friends. The sight of him makes my blood boil. I hope he goes tomorrow night. I really want to prove that my friends and I are brave, that we aren't to be messed with or picked on. I want to see him scared. And I want him to see us succeeding at something he can't.

". . . at your place?" I hear. It takes a moment to realize that Rohan is talking to me.

"What?" I ask, looking back at my new friends. "Sorry, zoned out again."

"I was asking if maybe we could hang out at your house," he says. "My place is too far away and neither of us has seen your place yet, so—"

"No," I say quickly.

"Oh," he responds. "Sorry, didn't mean to be rude by inviting myself over."

"It's not that," I reply. I lower my eyes and look to my snow boots. "It's just that my dad's been super busy lately, so the house is a pigsty. And he hasn't been to the grocery store in, like, weeks, so the only thing we have to eat is frozen fish sticks and instant mashed potatoes." My stomach lurches unpleasantly at the thought.

"That's okay," Mira says. "We can head to my house. I'll text my parents to make sure it's okay, but I doubt they'll mind."

She pulls out her phone and starts to text, but before she can get too far, a hand reaches out of the crowd and yanks the phone from her grasp.

"Hey!" she yelps.

But it's no use. It's Bradley, flanked by his two bully friends, Chet and Bo.

Bradley holds the phone up and out of her reach. Not that Mira actually reaches for it. Even Rohan says nothing; he looks at the bullies, clearly torn between wanting to stick up for the girl he has a crush on and worried he'll get his face beaten in. My hands clench into fists. I take a step forward, but Mira holds me back and Bo looks at me menacingly.

"Oooh, texting Mommy and Daddy," Bradley says tauntingly. "What should we write to them, boys?"

"That she thinks her mom is ugly," Bo suggests.

"Or that her dad smells like dog pee," Chet says.

"Please . . ." Mira whispers.

"I know," Bradley says, completely ignoring her. He starts typing. "How about: 'Dear Mom and Dad, I hate you both so much, and all I want for the holidays is to never see you again.'" He taps the screen victoriously. "Perfect! Sent!"

Finished, he tosses the phone to her. She grabs for it but fumbles; the phone falls to the ground with a *crack*.

"Oops," Bradley says with a cackle. "Hopefully your parents can afford a new phone. Though judging by your old one, I highly doubt it."

He high-fives Chet.

As they turn to go, still laughing, I step up to him and cut them off.

"Why are you like this?" I ask. I don't know where the words or the bravery comes from, but the moment I stand in front of him, I wish I could take it back.

He glares down at me.

For a moment, it looks like he's sizing me up, and I wonder if he'll punch me, just as easily as he would have punched Rohan. He doesn't seem like the type who would shy away from hitting girls.

Then his expression turns into a wicked smile.

"You haven't been here long enough to know how things run in this town. So I'll give you a pass, new girl." He takes a step toward me, forcing me to step back. "I'm like this because I *can* be. Who's going to stop me? You?"

He takes another step. I step to the side, because there's a look in his eyes that tells me I don't want to push him any further.

"That's what I thought," he says when I'm out of his way. "This is how things are in Gold River. Some kids are meant to rule this school. Some—like you and your friends—aren't."

He and his friends start walking away, but then he pauses.

"Unless," he says, looking over his shoulder at us,

"you three decide to grow backbones and actually show up tomorrow night. But I wouldn't, if I were you. This Dare is going to be special. It's the thirty-third anniversary of the Carlisle Massacre, and we're going to hold a séance to speak to the people who perished there. If you're not careful, you might join them."

Then he turns and walks away.

When they're out of earshot, Rohan asks, "What did he mean, *séance*?"

For the first time while talking about going to the Carlisle, he actually sounds scared.

"I don't know," Mira says. There are tears in her eyes, and she cradles her broken phone to her chest. "But I don't care. We're going tomorrow night. And we're going to be the last ones standing. No matter what."

4

That night, I dream of walking through the halls of the Carlisle.

Not just the stark, flickering hall leading to something terrible, but the guest hallways. The dream feels different tonight, and not just because it's a different scenario. My skin tingles. Like I'm being watched.

I wander past open doors. And inside every single one is a person, or a couple, or a family—men and women and children. All of them dressed like they're going to a fancy dinner.

All of them are dead.

I can see through them, all of them. They float back and forth in their rooms, but they don't come toward me as my feet guide me down the halls.

As if they're trapped in their rooms.

As if they're imprisoned.

As if they're waiting for someone—for *me*—to let them out.

Somewhere, deep down, I think I should help them. But I can't stop. My feet won't let me.

Soon, I reach the end of the hall, and I know if I turn left I will head toward the stairwell leading to the basement. To the flickering white hallway and its door of death.

I turn right.

To a short hallway.

To a closed door at the end.

Room 333.

My hand reaches out and turns the doorknob. It opens easily.

Like it's been waiting for me.

Inside, the room is empty.

And I know then that it's the only empty room in the entire hotel.

And I also know what the strange sensation is.

The hotel is hungry.

The hotel has a vacancy, and tomorrow night it plans on filling it.

5

I'm surprised by how many kids show up. It's ten o'clock, go time, and almost our entire seventh-grade class is arranged outside the massive double doors leading into the Carlisle. Everyone is huddled together like penguins, flashlights or cellphone lights gripped in trembling gloved hands. No one goes to the door to step inside. We're all waiting for something, but I don't know what.

Even though there's like forty kids out here, the night air is nearly silent. Mira keeps looking back toward the long, dark, winding drive we took to get here, undoubtedly worried to see the telltale streak of headlights as the cops—or worse, our parents—drive up the hill to bust us.

I just keep staring at the once-grand hotel billboard a few feet away from us, boldly claiming:

THE CARLISLE HOTEL
THE NATION'S PREMIER WINTER DESTINATION
~~NO~~ VACANCY

I don't know who crossed out the *no*, but just staring at it is ominous.

It reminds me of the dream, and the aching hunger the hotel seemed to have.

"I have everything we could possibly need," Rohan whispers, holding up his backpack and forcing my attention away from the darkness lingering in my mind. "An emergency blanket, spare flashlights and batteries, granola bars, juice boxes, cookies. And I made a thermos of hot chocolate before leaving."

"How in the world did you manage to make late-night hot chocolate without your parents noticing?" Mira asks.

He shrugs. "I made sure to make hot chocolate every night around nine-thirty for the last few weeks so it wouldn't seem out of the ordinary."

Mira raises an eyebrow at him. He grins sheepishly.

"Wow," I say. "You really have been preparing for this."

He nods, his cheeks flushing. "I've been waiting for tonight for the last few years. It's finally my chance to prove I'm not just a nerd."

Even though he's been the one pushing us to do this since I arrived in Gold River, my heart softens a bit. Especially when I look over and see Bradley and his gang standing a little farther off. Rohan isn't doing this because he wants to be popular or cool. He's doing this because he wants to feel safe.

And the only way to do that is to do something that feels entirely *un*safe.

From the corner of my eye, I see a girl step up in front of the doors. I've never seen her before. When she steps up, the entire crowd goes even more silent, like everyone's holding their breath. In that moment, I realize that I am, too.

"That's Leslie Chalmers," whispers Mira. "She's in high school. And she holds the record for longest time spent in the Carlisle—four a.m."

"Welcome seventh graders," Leslie says. Her

voice is clear and musical, and she stands there with her arms out and her head high. I wonder if she's in theater or something; she seems to radiate when she's the center of everyone's attention. She lowers her arms, and her expression turns wicked. "Welcome . . . to the last night of your childhood."

She gestures to the giant gilded doors behind her. "You know why you're here. The Carlisle Dare is the stuff of legends. So far, no one has lasted the entire night. Not even me." She shudders theatrically, though as we stand there, I notice Mira shivering as well, and think it might not all be for show. It's not just the cold, either; this place makes my skin feel electric and my pulse race in anticipation. Like Rohan, I feel like I've been waiting for this my entire life.

"As you know, it's against the rules for anyone to share what they experience during their stay in the Carlisle, but I can say this—what you'll find inside these doors is far worse than your darkest nightmares."

She pauses for dramatic effect, the sharp glare of a dozen flashlights making her face incredibly eerie. Another wave of chills races over my skin. As well as a jolt of excited adrenaline.

"The rules are simple: Once you walk inside these doors, there's no leaving. Not unless you want to be disqualified. The one who stays the longest wins. And tonight, we have a special treat. As if it wasn't scary enough, at midnight we are hosting a séance to connect to the souls who lost their lives here, thirty-three years ago to this very day."

As if on cue, something crashes within the hotel. Everyone jumps, including Leslie. And me.

Leslie laughs, but it's clear she was surprised. Something about her posture is guarded, flinching.

Scared.

I wonder what she experienced here.

I wonder if she's also nervous about going back inside.

"It looks like the ghosts are excited to have you," she says. "Well. Let's not keep them waiting."

She gestures, and two older kids from the crowd step forward and open the doors.

The dark lobby of the Carlisle Hotel stares out at us. Even from here, I swear I can smell the dust and decay and hunger. I look to my friends. Rohan's excitement has faded. He stands there, holding his thermos and flashlight, his breath coming out in rapid, short clouds. Only Mira looks remotely ready for what awaits us; she stares ahead with a determined look on her face. And me? There's an eagerness inside me. I should be scared like everyone else. But I'm not.

The crowd moves forward, herding us along.

We head inside.

I don't know what's creepier—the cavernous hotel or the feeling that I've been here before.

Beams from forty flashlights dance over the lobby, illuminating walls covered in molding art, faded red carpet that sweeps up a grand staircase the width of my house, and statues and concierge desks draped in dust and spiderwebs.

We huddle together in the darkness, which is made infinitely scarier by the frantic light beams. The shadows could be hiding anything, and it seems like no matter how fast we shine our lights, we can't keep the darkness at bay.

That darkness is hungry. I feel it in my bones, as if the whole hotel is breathing us in. Savoring our scent. Anticipating how we taste.

No one dares to speak, let alone breathe.

I pass my flashlight over a nearby statue

—and reveal a skeletal white face with snarling teeth only inches away from me.

"Bradley!" I yelp, my scream echoing out in the heavy silence. Everyone in the class looks over at my embarrassment, but that scream seems to break the spell. A few kids giggle—probably at me—and others begin to talk quietly among themselves.

Bradley cackles with glee and high-fives one of his friends as he steps back.

"I bet I know who's going home first!" he laughs. "You three won't even make it to the séance."

"We'll see about that," I growl under my breath. He's already walking away, completely ignoring me. To him, I know, my response isn't even worth hearing.

"You can't let him get to you so much," Mira says. She takes my hand as she says it, which I realize is clenched in a fist.

"Says you," I reply. I can't keep the anger out of my voice. I watch him and his cronies walk away;

they head up the staircase, still talking and laughing to themselves. "I thought he was the whole reason you decided to do this."

"He is," she admits. "But I try not to let him get under my skin. He's always been like this. To me and Rohan and everyone else he doesn't deem cool enough. That's why I'm here—to prove we *are* cool enough, both to him and to the rest of the school. This is how we beat them at their own stupid game."

I swallow down my anger. *You need to stop letting other people get to you,* my mom told me many times. *Everyone has an opinion. Those opinions don't matter unless you let them.*

"You're right," I say. "I won't let him get to me, but we *will* be the last ones standing. Promise?"

Mira smiles, as does Rohan.

"Promise," they say in unison.

"Now," Rohan continues, "let's go explore this bad boy."

Mira's smile slips instantly. "Wait, really? I thought we could just maybe stay here. You know, where it's safe."

"Where's the fun in that?" Rohan replies. He starts walking away, toward the staircase. Clearly he knows we'll follow. "Besides, everyone else is doing it."

And he's right. The rest of the class has already started walking away, heading down hallways or up the sweeping staircase.

Every single kid who leaves makes the lobby a little darker.

A little emptier.

Every kid who leaves makes the hotel feel even hungrier, as they walk deeper into its clutches. I can feel the hotel calling me. Drawing me in.

Jasmine, the hotel breathes.

I shudder.

Mira jumps and looks around.

"What?" I ask her.

"Did you hear that?" she asks.

I bite my tongue.

"Hear what?" I reply.

"I swear . . . no, it's nothing. Must be the wind. Or Bradley playing a trick." She shakes herself and starts walking toward Rohan, who's gesturing for us to hurry up.

In the deepening darkness, I don't want to wait. The more of us who stick together, the better.

"What was it?" I ask her in a whisper. "What did you hear?"

She looks to me. Then her eyes dart to the darkness surrounding us.

"I swear I heard someone calling my name," she replies. "I know it's silly, but it feels like the hotel has been waiting for me."

That's not silly, I think. *I feel it too.*

But I don't say anything as we near Rohan. I don't know if admitting that would make her feel better, or only scare her more.

The important thing is that we make it through tonight.

7

Even though I know the rest of our class is here with us, even though I've seen the beams of their flashlights darting down other hallways, it's impossible not to feel like the three of us are alone.

As we walk, I feel like I'm back in one of my dreams.

It's not a good feeling.

The upstairs is mostly halls of locked rooms. We creep slowly down them, our feet sinking softly on the ragged carpet, little clouds of dust and old spiderwebs puffing up with every step. The carpet is deep red, like blood, though faded and worn from years of neglect. The walls are a geometric print, pale beige, and large chunks of the paper peel down like strips of skin. Chandeliers hang darkly above us, their crystalline branches completely still and silent as we pass beneath them, our flashlights momentarily turning dripping diamonds into rainbows or disco balls. There are no windows here, and the darkness at both ends of the hall gives the illusion that there is nothing else before or behind us.

Just hallways.

Just darkness.

Halfway down one hall, Rohan stops in front of a door.

"What are you doing?" Mira whispers harshly.

He hesitates and looks over his shoulder at us.

"I want to see what's inside," he says. "Also, why are you whispering? Are you worried you'll wake the dead?"

"Not funny," Mira replies.

I put a hand on her shoulder. I don't want him to open it any more than she does; all I can think of is my latest dream, and the hundreds of ghostly occupants trapped in their rooms, waiting to be released. Waiting to torment the living.

"Maybe we should just leave it alone," I say. "It's probably locked anyway."

"Oh, come on, don't chicken out on me now. This is our one chance to explore this place. What else are we going to do until tomorrow?"

"Sit safely in the lobby and not disturb anything and win?" Mira asks. "Sounds like a solid plan to me."

"Me too," I reply. "What if there are, like, bodies or something in there?"

Rohan's hand goes to the doorknob. He grins wickedly. In that moment, he almost reminds me of Bradley. Almost.

"They wouldn't keep the bodies in here," Rohan says. "The police would have taken them away and buried them properly." His resolve seems to waver, though. His hand is on the doorknob, but he no longer seems so eager to open it. Clearly he hadn't considered there might be something—or some*one*— waiting behind it. "Even if they *were* still in there," he continues, trying to psych himself up, "they'd just be bones and dust."

He sighs. Then he drops his hand and hangs his head.

"Maybe you're right," he says. "Maybe we shouldn't do it. Just in case."

"Do what?" comes a very unwelcome voice behind us. Bradley.

He strolls down the hall with Bo and Chet in tow.

"Don't tell me you were debating going home already," he says when he nears. His smirk widens. "Or were you thinking of maybe moving in?" he asks, gesturing to the door. He looks at me. "I've driven by your house a couple times, Jasmine. The place is a dump. I bet even a run-down pit like this would seem like a palace to you." He chuckles. "You'd certainly fit right in."

"What's that supposed to mean?" My rage is rising. No one ever spoke to me like this in Florida. No one should be able to talk like this to someone *anywhere*.

"I mean you're trash," he says. "So this place is perfect for you." He shoves past Rohan, who stumbles to the ground. Mira rushes over to help him stand. I barely notice them. My vision has narrowed so much I can only see Bradley. "Why don't we check out your new room?" he asks. "Maybe you'll be lucky. Maybe you'll already have a roommate."

And without pause or worry about what horrors might be inside, he kicks open the door.

8

The door slams open so loudly, the walls shake.

Behind us, something crashes and shatters.

One of Bradley's friends—maybe Bo or Chet, I don't know—yelps in surprise. Instantly, we all turn toward the source of the crash, our flashlights darting down the hall.

A chandelier has fallen. It lies there, a mangled mess, its crystals scattered all over the floor like fallen stars. Even Bradley goes quiet at what he's done.

It's more than just vandalism: It feels like we've triggered something.

Awoken something.

Something we can't undo.

After a few moments of silence, when nothing comes out of the room to scream at us, and no adults thunder down the hall demanding we apologize for breaking a piece of history, Bradley scoffs.

"See what I mean?" he says. "Trash. Everything about this place is junk."

He glares his flashlight in my face, nearly blinding me.

"Must *really* feel like home now," he says.

I reach out and blindly try to shove the flashlight away, but he's already stepping into the empty room, Bo and Chet close behind him. I force down my rage and look to my friends, trying to take calming breaths.

"Are you okay?" I whisper to Rohan.

He nods. He's clearly shaken, but it's also clear that he doesn't want to seem like a coward in front of Bradley. Mira's eyes are wide. I can tell she wants to be anywhere but here, just as I hear her words echo in my head: *Don't let him get under your skin.*

Too late.

We follow Bradley and his friends into the hotel room.

The room. Is. Huge.

Like, easily the size of our classroom, with a king-size bed and thick crimson curtains and an armoire as wide as I am tall. And everything—*everything*—is covered in dust. It's so thick it's impossible to tell what the carpet color is, or what the pattern on the bed-spread might be. With every step we take in the room, small clouds of dust billow up, dancing in the beams of our flashlights.

I'm glad I'm wearing a scarf—a gift from my mother—and see I'm not the only one burying my face in wraps of fabric. It feels like inhaling the dust of corpses.

Bradley's flashlight trails over the walls—bland paintings of alpine flowers and pine trees and skis—and reflects off the large oval mirror above a wooden desk. He pokes his head in the bathroom, Bo and Chet right behind him.

"Nothing in there," he says. He steps out into the main room. Rohan and Mira and I have barely moved past the entry. I keep remembering the dream, the ghosts trapped in these rooms. I keep waiting for them to appear.

For them to make us one of them.

"Ugh," Bradley says, wiping a cobweb onto Bo's shoulder. "This place is disgusting. This whole thing is such a waste of time. I can't believe anyone would find this scary."

He walks toward us, past the mirror, and I see it—
a pale white face in the reflection,
a gaunt, skeletal grimace,
with sharpened teeth
and hollow black eyes, staring at him

                    with its mouth

                    wide

                    open

                    in a scream

                    or

                    a devouring

                      hunger.

Bradley pushes past me, and I blink.

When I look back to the mirror, the apparition is gone.

The goose bumps over my skin are not.

Bradley stomps down the hall with his friends, but I can't turn away. I keep staring at the mirror, waiting for the ghost to appear again. My feet are frozen to the floor.

I wasn't imagining that, right?

A hand on my shoulder makes me jump.

"Are you okay?" Rohan asks. It's then that I realize I'm not the only one standing stock-still. Mira is beside me, staring at the mirror with the same look of fear.

"Did you . . . did you see that?" she whispers.

"See what?" Rohan asks. He looks around the empty room, instantly on high alert. "I didn't see anything. What did you see?"

"A ghost," I answer. "It was right here. Right behind Bradley. I saw it in the mirror."

"Me too," Mira replies. She looks at me, her eyes wide with fear. "Maybe this place really is haunted."

I nod.

Rohan grumbles about feeling left out.

"Trust me," Mira says. "You don't want to see it. Come on, let's get out of here. It creeps me out."

She turns and heads out the room, Rohan at her side.

I linger there for a moment, watching the shadows. I swear I see the palest bleed of white in the corner.

A face, watching me.

Despite myself, my lips twitch into a grin.

This might end up being a creepy night after all; now, if only I could get Bradley to see what I do.

9

Mira and Rohan and I wander the halls of the Carlisle Hotel on our own after that. Even though we occasionally catch sight of flashlights at the end of a hall, or hear voices coming around a corner (every time, we freeze, wide-eyed, before recognizing the voices of our classmates), it feels like we have the entire hotel to ourselves. The place is so monstrously massive, it's easy to feel like nothing exists outside of here. Like the halls of this place could go on forever. Hours pass like it's nothing.

We wander into a huge room that was clearly the

swimming pool. The pool itself is drained and easily the size of our entire gym, with dozens of spiderweb-covered lounge chairs arranged around the edge. Some of them are still draped with towels, the edges threadbare and ragged, like the clothes of corpses. I can just imagine the huge windows all along one side would give a perfect view of the ski slopes beyond. The place still smells vaguely of chlorine.

When we turn to go, I swear I hear kids splashing and laughing behind us. I square my shoulders and ignore it.

We pass by enormous dining rooms. The crisp white tablecloths are covered with dust, but our flash-lights still glint over perfectly set china, the whole place waiting for a dinner that never occurred.

"What do you think happened to everyone?" Rohan asks as we make our way through the maze of round tables. His flashlight alights on a bowl in the center of one table. Dinner rolls still fill it to the brim, somehow untouched by age. When he picks one up and knocks it on the table, it's hard as a rock. "I know the reports say everyone died, but how? It's almost like they all vanished."

I glance around at the empty room. It's far too easy to imagine a hundred diners in here in their fancy clothes. Far too easy to hear the faint clink of cutlery, the low murmur of voices, the beautiful swells of the string quartet playing on the raised stage in the corner.

I close my eyes. I swear I can actually hear the guests, the music, the clink of silverware. I swear, when I open my eyes, the dining room will actually be full. The presence fills me, takes over. I stretch out my arms, feeling my body moving to music from decades ago.

"Hey, Jasmine," Rohan says.

I open my eyes, and I'm in the empty dining room, standing with my arms outspread and a contented smile on my face.

"Are you feeling okay?" he asks.

I drop my arms.

"Yeah," I say, trying to think fast. "Just can't believe how big this space is, you know? Trying to take it all in."

He raises an eyebrow.

"Riiiight," he says.

I glance over to see Mira wearing a similarly confused expression.

Before either of them can grill me further, Rohan's watch beeps. Immediately, his eyes light up with excitement.

"It's séance time."

10

Most of the kids are gathered in the lobby when we get there.

Most of them.

There are clearly fewer than there were gathered at the beginning. Maybe only thirty remaining now. I wonder what scared them off. I wonder if they saw what we've seen in the mirror.

They've formed a ring around a fire pit someone has dragged in, and a good fifty candles are dotted around the room, dripping down the staircase or perched atop marble statues. The light flickers on my classmates' faces, casting shadows that dart and dance on the crimson carpet. Like their spirits are trapped and straining to break free. Or like dark entities are hovering just behind them, waiting to pounce. Despite all the candles and fire, the room feels even colder than the rest of the hotel.

In the center of the ring, facing the fire pit, is Leslie, the girl who lasted almost the entire night.

Rohan and Mira and I walk quietly down the steps and take our places in the ring.

I glance around. Bradley and his cronies stand across from us. Bradley sticks out his tongue when he sees me looking. I take a deep breath and look away. *We'll see who's laughing when the morning comes.*

We stand there in silence for a while. Leslie keeps checking her phone for the time. After a handful of stragglers come and take their places in the circle, Leslie raises her hands.

"The midnight hour is here at last. You are the brave few who have made it this far," Leslie says, her voice echoing in the empty lobby. "You've explored the abandoned halls and peered into the darkness. But now it's time to invite the darkness to peer back."

Chills creep down my neck, and I'm not the only kid to shudder.

I look around the circle, staring past the faces of my classmates to the halls and corners beyond. In the fragile firelight, the darkness seems heavier, hungrier. It waits with sharpened claws, ready for the light to go out.

Ready to be invited in.

And that, I know, is precisely what Leslie is about to do.

The moment I think it, the chills turn to a sort of electricity. It simmers on my skin, prickling like plunging cold hands into warm water. It's almost sort of pleasant.

"Please join hands," Leslie says. There's a shuffle as kids nervously take the hands of their neighbors. No one says a word. Mira squeezes my hand tight; Rohan's fingers tremble against mine, and I can't tell if it's from fear or excitement. His face is obscured by his hood, and besides, I can't take my eyes off Leslie.

She closes her eyes and tilts her head back. When she speaks again, her voice is louder, stronger.

"Spirits!" she calls. "We summon thee! On this night, the thirty-third anniversary of your demise, we call to you. Stir from your slumber. Tell us your tales. Speak, O spirits. Speak!"

The electricity in me rises. Vibrates in my skin and muscles and bones. My hands shake, or maybe my friends' hands shake. The fire in front of Leslie crackles higher, and the candles around us flicker in a breeze that shouldn't exist.

Leslie howls with laughter, and cries out again: "Rise, O spirits! Rise, Grand Dame! We call on you to complete your work! On this, the cursed night, we call on you to rise. Rise, and work your magic. Rise, and let the dead walk again! Come to us, Grand Dame, we call to thee! We summon thee! We offer ourselves to thee!"

"What?" Mira asks beside me. "What is she talking about?"

But I can barely hear her. Because the moment Leslie is done calling out, the hotel responds.

Wind howls around us, swirling around the circle, carrying the cackles and screams of three hundred lost souls.

Candle flames whip and flare bright and blaze out, wax flicking against the floor and walls and statues like splatters of blood.

The central fire pit billows up, burning so bright and hot that we all take a step back, shielding our faces against the blinding light. Leslie screams and runs, hiding behind a statue. But I'm not paying attention to her.

I'm paying attention to the face that appears in the fire.

The fire that's turning a deep, vibrant purple.

Two sharp green eyes slice through the flames, along with dark lips of smoke that smile and somehow brim with spite.

"*Stupid children,*" the voice cackles. A woman's voice. A voice that makes the electricity in my bones jump to full blast, a voice that makes my very nerves vibrate. "*Playing with powers you cannot comprehend. Insulting those who came before you. I, the Grand Dame, hope you have enjoyed your little games. Because tonight will be your last!*"

The fire explodes. My classmates scream out and scatter.

But I, like Mira, am frozen to the spot. The room fades around me, the screams muted, the slamming doors and windows distant. The electricity is a hum, a noise, like a thousand angry bees in my skull.

I feel my toes lift off the ground.

I feel Mira—our hands still clutched—rise beside me.

Then the buzzing becomes too much, and darkness overtakes me.

II

Voices murmur around me. Three hundred voices.

"Is it her? Can it be?"

And another.

The Grand Dame.

"*She is here,*" she says. "*She has come at last. We have the girl, and she will set us free!*"

I feel her eyes on me. Feel her come close in the darkness.

Feel her words sink through my skull as she peers deep into my thoughts, as she unravels all my secrets.

The Grand Dame speaks to me, and when she does, my whole world burns.

My head sloshes and shifts like a ship in a stormy, midnight sea. Voices ebb and roar in the heavy black. But they are jumbled now, churning with the waves as I rock back and forth, back and forth, and above me the stars blink in and out—

I blink, and it's not stars above me anymore, but flashlights. The voices come from my worried friends; Rohan and Mira kneel beside me.

Wait. How did I end up on the floor?

"What—" I begin, but Mira pats my shoulder.

"Shh, it's okay," she whispers. But even though I'm feeling out of it, I hear the tremble in her words. The unintentional slip that nothing is okay at all.

"What happened?" I ask. My words are thick in my mouth, like I drank a whole tube of honey.

Mira and Rohan share a glance.

"You . . . you fainted," Rohan says.

"Fainted?" comes another voice. A very unwelcome voice. "She screamed like a baby and passed out."

"Go away, Bradley," Mira says.

"Or what?" he asks.

I turn my head—I still don't feel like I can sit up—to see him standing beside us, with Bo and Chet flanking him. But he doesn't look as calm and mean as he usually does.

Like Rohan and Mira, he looks scared. Even Chet's and Bo's eyes dart around the room like they're waiting to be ambushed.

"Just go," says another voice. I turn my head the other way and see Leslie, the girl who did the séance, standing over me. "Go be useful. Maybe one of you meatheads can get the doors to open."

Wait, what?

The jolt of confusion gives me the energy to finally push myself up to sitting.

The lobby is in chaos.

The candles have all gone out, and the central fire pit has been reduced to coals that lie scattered and smoldering. Kids huddle close to one another, their flashlights flickering all over the room. Some stand back-to-back, as if they're afraid of something sneaking up behind them. Others stand near the main doors.

No.

They're *banging* on the doors. And the windows. The thuds of their fists against the wood and glass echo through the hallway. Others try even more drastic approaches, swinging coatracks or statues at the windows.

Judging from the frustrated yells and crying, it doesn't seem to be working.

"What happened?" I ask again, more forcefully this time.

"Maybe you should ask Leslie," Mira says. No mistaking the note of anger in her voice.

Leslie clears her throat.

"The séance worked," she says sheepishly.

"I'd say!" Mira replies, her voice squeaking. "You let out all the ghosts and trapped us in here!"

"I didn't—"

"What?" I gasp.

Mira grunts and looks back to me.

"Leslie's little séance worked, Jasmine. The moment you started screaming, the hotel went . . . *funny*. The windows shook and there was a sound like ghosts and the statues moved and the chandeliers spun and that face . . ." She shudders. "That terrible face said she was the Grand Dame, and that we would be trapped here forever. And then . . ." She stops herself. "Then the fire went out."

"Now we're stuck," Rohan says. "The doors are locked and the windows won't break. And none of us have any cellphone service."

Out of habit, I reach into my pocket and pull out my phone. No bars.

"How is this even possible?" I ask.

Mira points to Leslie. "Ask her. She's the one who summoned the Grand Dame."

"I didn't know it would work," Leslie mutters. And even though she's older than all of us, in that moment, she looks horribly young. She shakes her head. "I was just coming over to make sure she was okay—"

"*No thanks to you,*" Mira mutters.

Leslie ignores her. "But I'm going to try the door again. We need to band together. We can't let ourselves fall apart."

She leaves us, so it's just Mira and Rohan and me, sitting there on the faded, dusty carpet, the darkness eating hungrily at the edges. The voices I'd heard while passed out sift through my thoughts. What was that?

"Come on," Rohan says. He stands and helps me

up. "Let's go help the others. Maybe we can break down the door with a statue or something. Use it like a battering ram."

I nod. My thoughts are slow. I just keep thinking what Mira said: *The séance worked. The séance worked.*

Rohan heads over to the door, but Mira pulls me to the side.

"I heard something," she whispers. "When you started screaming, right before you passed out, the voice . . ." She shudders again. "The Grand Dame said something about having the girl." Her eyes go wide. "You don't think . . . you don't think she meant you, do you? I mean, you fainted . . ."

I feel the color leave my cheeks. My heart races. She heard the Grand Dame, too. After someone. After a girl. After me? What did it all mean?

I swallow hard.

"Come on," I say. "Let's see if we can get out of here."

We have the girl. We have the girl. She will set us free.

I know then that none of us are getting free. At least, none of us living kids.

The only ones getting out of here tonight are the ghosts that have been trapped in the hotel.

And they've been waiting thirty-three years to do it.

12

We manage to get a couple of the kids to help us topple an old marble statue and use it as a battering ram. It took convincing, since apparently most of them expected it to reach out and grab them. But after poking it a few times to no effect, they give in. I feel bad as we tilt the priceless piece of art to the side, and have to bite my tongue so I don't yell out not to break it. Because no one will know. No one has been in here, and unless we do something, we aren't getting out.

But even with all our strength, and no matter how hard we hit the wooden doors, the statue just bounces back. Like it's made of rubber and the doors are solid steel.

After a few tries, we let the statue drop and collapse back, exhausted. I watch a few of my classmates chucking whatever they can find at the enormous windows. The glass doesn't break, either.

I check my phone once more. It's still without signal, and the batteries are draining unnaturally fast. I mentally kick myself for not bringing a spare charger. At least Rohan brought extra flashlight batteries. At this rate, we're going to need them.

"Okay," Leslie says. She paces back and forth, illuminated by an electric lantern on the ground. "We need to get everyone gathered together. Stick to the same room. Whatever's happening, our parents will notice if we're still gone by morning. They'll come looking for us. They'll see our footprints and find us here."

"Actually—" comes a girl's voice by the window. "I don't think they will."

We huddle up to the other window and look out, shining our flashlights into the thick snow.

"That's impossible," Rohan whispers.

Because as we watch, the hundreds of footsteps

and yards of trampled snow outside the hotel begin to disappear. One footprint at a time, as though someone is *un*walking, the footprints vanish. In a matter of moments, all the footsteps are gone, replaced by clean, smooth snow.

To make matters worse, the moment the footsteps clear, it begins to snow.

Hard.

"About that," Mira says.

Leslie shakes her head and steps back. "This can't be happening. This can't be real."

"But you said all those things about this place being haunted," Rohan says.

"I didn't mean them!" Leslie replies. Her eyes are wide. "Every year the upperclassmen get you guys to come and stay the night. Most of the kids freak themselves out just because it's cold and dark. And the ones who stick around get scared off because the upperclassmen come along and dress up as ghosts and try to scare them. I never saw any real ghosts when I was here, but the kids scared me away. It was always just a trick. It was never real!"

"So maybe we just wait until the older kids show up," I say. I don't know where the confidence comes from. "If they're going to come along and try to scare us, maybe they'll be able to help instead."

But Leslie shakes her head.

"They were supposed to get here before the start of the séance. They were going to hide out and bang on the windows. But they never showed. I kept texting them, but they didn't write back."

"That's why you were checking your phone," Mira says.

Tears fill Leslie's eyes. She nods.

"Okay, well," Rohan says, "if we all just stick together in here, eventually someone will come and find us. Right? We just have to make sure no one leaves this room for any reason."

At that moment, a scream cuts through the room, making my blood go cold.

Everyone looks
             to see one of our classmates
                              floating,
                              wrapped in
                              black
                                 shadowy
                                    vines,
             at the top of the staircase.

"Martin!" someone calls.

The boy cries out again.

He struggles against the shadows that bind him, but he can't break free.

That strange static fills my veins again, makes my fingers shake.

"Help me!" he screams.

Two burning green eyes appear in the shadow, along with the sharp, smiling lips of the Grand Dame.

Martin cries out again, and then the shadow wraps around him, dragging him deep into the bowels of the hotel.

13

The room erupts into chaos.

My classmates scream in terror, but it's not just from Martin's disappearance. No. Other shadows whip from the corners of the room, wrapping around kids and pulling them away. As we watch, huddled beside the door, ghostly shapes appear in the dark. Pale spirits with terrible faces, sharp teeth, and blank eyes. They billow from the walls, glide down the stairs, wailing horribly.

They chase our classmates out of the lobby and into the waiting halls.

Doors slam and statues crash in the wake of their panic.

"We have to get out of here," Leslie says as, around us, more ghosts seep from the shadows, and the chandelier above us sways dangerously.

"But you said to stick together and stay here!" Mira replies.

Before they can argue further, the statue lying on the ground between us begins to shake.

Begins to move.

Cracks form in the marble, and its head jerks around to face us. Its pale eyes burn green, and when it opens its cracked lips, its teeth are obsidian razors.

"Run!" Rohan yells.

He doesn't need to say it twice. The four of us take off at full speed, running from the statue that sprouts another set of spiderlike arms. I glance behind us as we tear toward a hallway. The statue transforms into a monstrous spider, all cracked white limbs and jagged fangs.

It scurries straight toward us.

We run.

We head toward the stairs, but the sinuous

handrail lifts from its pegs as we near, the end of it twisting into a hissing snake's head.

"This way!" I call, and dart down a hallway.

I hear my classmates farther ahead; their screams echo down the hall, along with the slam of doors as they try to find somewhere safe. I glance over my shoulder. The spider statue is gaining on us, its legs clacking on the floor before it scuttles, impossibly, up the wall and along the ceiling. Its fangs drip black saliva on the carpet, leaving steaming spots in its wake.

It's getting close.

So close.

I yank open the nearest door. Leslie and Mira and Rohan rush inside, and we slam the door shut behind us, leaning against it heavily.

Seconds later, the marble spider pounds against the door.

The wood shudders. Rohan yelps in fear.

Again.

And again.

The spider propels itself against the door.

Trying to break it down.

Trying to sneak inside to devour us.

"Let me in, little children," the statue calls in a gravelly, feminine voice—one that sounds far too similar to the Grand Dame's in the flames——*"I only want to play with you. We have so many games to play tonight, and we were only just beginning."*

"Go . . . go away!" I manage. I don't know where the words come from. My chest is constricted and I feel my heart beating in my throat, but the demand comes from nowhere. Though it almost sounds like a plea.

The thudding stops.

Instantly, the room is cavernously quiet. So quiet I can hear my breath, and my friends' breaths. Even the distant screams or crashing of my classmates is gone.

The room itself seems to breathe.

We stand there for what feels like hours. Waiting in the pitch black. Our flashlights illuminating small patches on the floor.

No one dares to move.

"Is it . . . is it gone?" Leslie whispers.

"Do you want to check?" Mira asks her.

Leslie shakes her head.

We wait there for a few more moments. There's no more slamming against the door.

Then again, I never heard the statue scuttle away, either.

I can just imagine it, waiting stoically on the other side of the door. Not needing to breathe. Not needing to shift. It's a statue, after all—it can outwait all of us.

"We should try to find another way out," I whisper.

Slowly, inch by inch, I shift my weight from the door. The others do the same.

"Where are we, anyway?" Rohan asks.

He moves his flashlight from the carpet and scans the room. I don't take my eyes off the door handles. At any moment I expect the marble spider to crash against the door again, to have to slam our bodies against it to keep us from getting overtaken.

"Um, guys?" Rohan whispers. His voice shakes. "You might want to see this."

I turn around and shine my light about the room. It's a huge space—the size of our gym. Huge and empty.

But something seems strange.

That's when my flashlight catches on an object a few feet away from me.

I thought it was a bare table.

Not a table.

A chandelier.

I glance at Rohan, whose flashlight is trained to the ceiling. I follow the beam.

To see all the dining room tables perched *above* us.

14

Leslie immediately collapses to the floor.

I mean, ceiling.

She covers her head in her hands and starts rocking back and forth.

"This can't be happening, this can't be happening," she whispers.

Mira, at least, seems to be taking it a little bit better. "What did you *think* would happen?" she asks, circling her flashlight around the ceiling. Her light glints off the cutlery and plates and expensive glasses. My eyes catch on the knives. Did that one just move?

"Not *this*," Leslie says.

"Then why—"

"There's no use arguing about it," I say. "I mean, come on—we've all done silly things like trying to get Bloody Mary to come out of a mirror, you know? No one really expects them to work. She didn't mean for all of this to happen."

Leslie's eyes glint with tears when she looks at me. *Thank you,* she mouths.

I kneel down beside her.

"Who gave you the idea of the séance, anyway?" I ask.

"I don't know," she admits.

"What do you mean you don't know?" Mira asks.

"I mean, I got an email. I didn't recognize the sender. It was all anonymous. I figured it was an upperclassman covering their tracks. And it just said to do the séance at midnight and say those words because it would really scare everyone."

"They weren't wrong," Rohan mutters.

I sigh.

"So we're stuck in here, and we don't know why," I say. "All we know is that *someone* wanted you to do the séance. They must have known what would happen."

"I bet it was Bradley," Rohan says. "He's enough of a jerk to do something like that."

"Why would he do that if he's trapped, too?" I ask.

Rohan shrugs. "Maybe it backfired."

"Maybe," I say. "But that still doesn't answer *why* we're trapped, or who the Grand Dame is, or how we're getting out of here before something worse happens."

"Speaking of," Mira says. "Is it feeling a little warm to you?"

I look over to see her tugging off her scarf. Rohan, too, is shuffling in his layers, unzipping his coat and pulling off his hat, his dark hair matted. I'd been so distracted—or else my coat was so good at keeping out both the cold *and* the heat—that I hadn't even noticed, but she's right. I peel off my gloves. The air is warm. Like, early summer warm. Did someone turn on the heat?

Reluctantly, I start undoing all my layers, leaving just a sweater and jeans and my scarf. Leslie does the same. And as we take off our heavy winter clothes, another change happens.

The lights in the inverted chandeliers flicker on.

Above us, fires roar to life in the massive fire-places, and the glass votives on the tables begin to glow. Their flames trail down, toward us, and just staring at the way the fire defies physics sends a whole new wave of vertigo through me. I reach out and hold on to the wall for support as the upside-down dining room glows warmly.

As the room comes to life.

"Whoa," Rohan whispers. He stares up at the ceiling, or the floor—*whichever*—entranced.

Distantly, I swear I hear the faint music of a string quartet.

"We should find the other kids," Leslie says. She pushes herself to standing, rolling her shoulders back. Clearly trying to take control of the strange situation and fix the mess she made, even if she didn't mean to make it.

She takes a few uncertain steps into the room.

Mira takes my hand and helps me to stand. Rohan waits expectantly a few feet away from us.

Leslie almost reaches the chandelier when we hear it.

Clank.

We all look toward the door. But the sound isn't

coming from there. It isn't from the beast outside.

No.

Something glitters on the ground between Leslie and Rohan and Mira and me.

A knife.

"What the . . ." Mira begins.

Another clank cuts her off.

The fork that fell wobbles only an inch from her feet, the prongs embedded in the ground.

We all glance up.

To see the cutlery beginning to hover over the tables.

Another fork falls down toward us. And another. And another.

"Run!" I yell.

But Leslie can't run. Because now, she begins to hover above the ground. She yells out in fear as forks and knives fall around her, and she starts falling *up*.

Mira and I huddle against the wall, and a moment later, Rohan's feet begin to lift off the ground as well.

"Rohan!" Mira yells out.

She grabs my hand and takes a step forward. As I cling feebly to the doorknob, she stretches out, toward Rohan. His feet are inches off the floor now, and his eyes are wide with fear. Beyond him, over his shoulder, I watch as Leslie floats higher, and knives and cutlery fall around her like glittering, dangerous snow. She tries to swim through the air, tries to grab on to the chandelier as Mira finally latches onto Rohan's hand.

"Help me!" Leslie calls out. "Please!"

But there's no helping her. She's too far away.

Mira's grip tightens painfully on my hand as she struggles to hold on to Rohan. He grabs her hand with both of his and tries to pull himself toward us.

Behind him, Leslie twists and rotates slowly. She's nearly to the top, could reach out and touch a table if she tried.

Mira's grip on my hand strains. I look down to see that she, too, is starting to lift off the ground.

"No!" I yell out.

As Mira's fingers slip through mine.

As Rohan yells in fear.

As Leslie reaches the ceiling, and her feet touch.

The moment she's standing, it's like gravity snaps.

Instantly, Rohan and Mira collapse back to the ground, and the final pieces of cutlery clatter to the floor in front of us.

"Ow!" Rohan yelps, landing on his knees. Mira manages to land a little more gracefully.

Leslie, however, is still stuck on the ceiling.

"Um, guys?" she calls out. "How am I—"

But she doesn't get to finish what she was saying.

The lights around us snuff out, the whole room going pitch-black.

Someone screams.

A moment later, the lights flicker back on.

Mira and Rohan and I stand, surrounded by tables, the chandelier above us and all the cutlery set at its proper place. Just as it should be.

Like nothing ever happened.

Except Leslie is nowhere to be found.

15

"What . . . where . . . ?" Mira stammers. "Where did she go?"

She stumbles around the tables, peeking under the white tablecloths as if expecting Leslie to be hiding beneath them. Rohan doesn't leave my side; it's clear he's terrified that he'll be lifted off the ground again. I can only stand there in shock while Mira looks for Leslie.

Because in the dark, right before the light, I thought I saw two green eyes staring at me. I thought I'd caught the faint trace of perfume.

The Grand Dame.

She was here.

Watching.

Smiling.

Trying to get us alone.

She was succeeding.

"I don't think Leslie's still in here," I say, staring into the corners of the room, waiting to catch sight not of my classmate, but the Grand Dame.

"Then we have to find her!" Mira replies, panicked.

Panic is the last thing we need right now, but I know saying that will only upset her more. No one likes being told to calm down.

Rohan finally shakes himself from his fear and takes a few tentative steps over to her. When it's clear he isn't going to start floating again, he goes and puts a hand on her shoulder.

"It's going to be okay," he says. "Leslie's smart. And she's been in here before—she knows her way around. She'll be fine."

Mira doesn't seem to be listening. She reaches into Rohan's pocket and pulls out his phone, tapping the screen.

"Ugh!" she growls. She hands it back to him. "Still no service."

"At least the lights are still on?" I say, stepping over to them. "And it's warm. That has to be a good thing."

Mira looks at me like I'm losing my mind.

"What?" I ask, throwing up my arms. "We're trapped in a haunted hotel, and the only person who potentially knew what caused all of this is missing. I'm just trying to keep myself from losing it."

"But she didn't know," Mira says quietly. "The email was sent anonymously."

I consider, and remember what my friend had said earlier. "I think you were right," I admit, looking at Rohan. "I think it might have been Bradley."

"I knew it!" Rohan cheers.

"But why?" Mira asks. "Why would he have her do the séance if he knew it would do all this? He's trapped in here with us."

I shrug. "Think about it: He's admitted he pretty much owns this town. If anyone has access to secret histories about this place, it would be him. He probably didn't think it would work. Maybe he just read about it in some old book of his parents' and thought it would be enough to scare everyone away." I raise an eyebrow. "Because honestly? I don't think he's that tough or brave. I bet you anything that he was worried he wouldn't be strong enough to last the night. He probably thought the séance would be a surefire way to scare everyone out of the hotel quickly, so he could leave before he got scared himself."

"I don't know . . ."

"Come on, Mira," Rohan continues for me. "I know you don't like hating anybody, but he's the biggest jerk in town. And he kept dropping all those hints about this being the scariest night ever. He knew more than anyone else in our school. Besides, who *else* would want to do something this twisted? If anyone in Gold River is evil, it's him, and you know it. This is totally something he'd do."

She opens her mouth, then closes it. "You have a point," she mutters. She reaches back and touches her hair, as if unconsciously feeling for the fries he'd tossed at her in school.

"Right?" I say. "I say we go find him. If he read about the séance somewhere, maybe he knows how to, like, undo it or something."

"What about Leslie?"

I pause, then say, "I want to look for her. Really. But I think it's better if we do it as a big group. If the three of us run off on our own, we might get taken like she was, and then we can't help anybody. First, we look for Bradley and his goons. We can gather up other kids along the way. Then we undo the séance, and maybe if we're lucky, we'll run into Leslie, too. I bet she was just transported to another part of the hotel."

I can tell Mira isn't quite buying it, but she doesn't come up with any alternatives, either.

"What if the Grand Dame has her?" Mira whispers.

This time, it's my turn to be speechless.

"What do you think she wants?" Mira continues. "Why do you think the Grand Dame is doing this?"

Blink.

And I'm back in the hallway.

Orchestral music playing softly behind me.

Lights flickering above.

And in front of me, the door.

In front of me, the scent of her perfume, pulling me forward.

"We have her. We have her . . ."

I shake my head. The dream fades, but the vertigo does not.

Neither does the lingering scent of the Grand Dame's perfume.

Familiar. So familiar.

Mira looks at me, clearly concerned.

"I don't know why she'd do this," I say. "I don't know what any of this is about."

But I remember the hallway.

I remember the pull.

I remember the knowledge that death waited beyond that door.

And I have a terrible feeling I know *exactly* why we are here.

The hotel is hungry.

And we aren't leaving here until it's fed.

16

We leave through a different door—none of us want to find out if the spidery statue is still waiting for us to emerge—and find ourselves in the kitchen.

A small part of me had hoped we would find Leslie waiting on the other side—or even another one of our classmates. But the kitchen is empty.

Or at least, I think it is.

I *hope* it is.

It looks different now that the lights are on. Cleaner. Newer. But somehow even more menacing than in the dark.

Light glints off the steel countertops and shiny

appliances. Enormous empty pots and pans dangle from hooks, while rows of knives glitter dangerously on the walls. The fridges are massive, the size of closets, and the cabinets could be hiding anything. It's too bright. Too sterile. As if the kitchen itself is waiting for the ingredients to arrive so it can begin preparing its next meal.

I have a horrible feeling those ingredients include me and my classmates.

We take a hesitant step farther into the kitchen. Unlike the dining room, the air in here is refrigerator-cold. I wrap my arms around my chest, trying to stay warm.

Five steps in, and something crashes in the far corner, a metallic clang that nearly makes me yelp. We go stock-still and stare, eyes wide, trying to find what made the noise.

Silence.

"Should we go back?" Rohan whispers after a few terrified breaths.

I shake my head. We know the statue is waiting in the other direction. The only way out is forward.

Besides, maybe it was just a natural occurrence.

An old hook breaking or gravity toppling a bowl or something.

Yeah. That has to be it.

We keep walking toward the far door.

Past the gas ranges with the massive pots that could fit any one of us.

Past the cooking utensils that look like medieval torture devices.

Past the steel cupboards that reflect our terrified faces—

I stop dead.

The reflection in the cupboard isn't my own.

The Grand Dame stares back at me—a beautiful woman with long black hair and violent green eyes and red lips. She wears a long black dress with a cowl of black fur, and tiny glittering diamonds are studded through her hair. When she sees me staring at her, she smiles.

My vision shifts.

And I stand in the middle of the dining room. The tables are filled with guests, all of them dressed in their finest evening wear—smart tuxedos and elegant dresses—and their chatter intermingles with the music from the four-piece orchestra playing in the corner of the stage. Candles glitter warmly, and the chandeliers cast everything in a magical glow. Evergreen garlands drape across the walls and snow-flecked windows, while sprigs of mistletoe and poinsettias decorate the tables. There's a sort of electricity in the air and the conversation, an expectant energy. And when the woman in black ascends to the stage, it's clear she is the center of it.

The orchestra and conversation cut off at the same moment that she turns around.

The Grand Dame.

She smiles and sweeps her hands out to the sides.

"Welcome, my friends," she says. She doesn't raise her voice, but it somehow carries to all four corners of the room. Even in the vision, it sends a warm wave of energy down my spine. I can't look away. She exudes power and control. *"The night of communing is at hand. Tonight, all our work comes to fruition. All thanks to our very special guest. Come, child. Let us thank you."*

She reaches out her hand.

Toward me.

I look around.

Everyone in the room is staring at me.

I don't want to move, but my feet yank forward. I stumble toward the stage. Toward the Grand Dame. My heart hammers in my chest. I can't tell if it's from excitement or fear.

In no time at all I stand beside the Grand Dame. Her perfume is overpowering. But there's something else. A power that makes me sway just being in her presence. If not for her gloved hand on my shoulder, I would have fallen over.

"Let us have a round of applause for our guest of honor. Everyone? Show your appreciation for Sarah."

Sarah?

The crowd bursts into applause. They stand, clapping wildly, while the quartet begins playing triumphant music at my side. Confetti rains down from the ceiling. It's then that I notice some of the guests are crying.

"Take a bow, Sarah," the Grand Dame says. Her fingertips squeeze into my shoulder. I swear her nails draw blood. *"Enjoy this night. It's the only one you have left."*

She forces me down into a bow.

I look to my sneakers. Pale yellow hair falls past my face, bits of metallic confetti caught in the waves. Those aren't my shoes.

That isn't my hair.

I'm not Sarah. I'm . . .

"Jasmine?"

I jolt back and slam into the cupboard behind me. The noise is enough to raise the dead.

And when the cupboard at my back shakes and presses against me, I worry I've done just that.

17

I scream as the cupboard door behind me flies open, pushing me to my knees.

But it's not a skeleton or ghost or demon waiting inside.

It's one of our classmates. A boy named Jacob.

Jacob doesn't seem to realize it's us at first. He cowers against the cupboards, his eyes wide and slightly bloodshot. And it's only then, once I've scrambled to my feet, that I realize he looks like he's been through a war. His clothes are dusty, and the knees of his jeans are worn out. His hair is a mess.

"Jacob?" I ask. I take a step toward him. He

flinches back, causing the metal bowls on the counter behind him to topple with a loud crash. "Are you okay?"

Finally, he seems to come to his senses. His whole body shakes, and his eyes focus on me, then on Mira and Rohan.

Instantly, he lets out a relieved yell and runs forward, practically leaping into Mira's arms. She stumbles backward and hugs him, her eyebrows raised in confusion.

"Thank goodness it's you," he sobs. "I thought I was the only one left. It's been so long . . ." And then, Jacob starts to cry.

Mira and I share a look. She pats Jacob on the back awkwardly. As far as I know, they've never really talked to each other, but he acts as though she's his best, long-lost friend. Rohan stares at the kid like he's worried Jacob has lost his mind.

"What are you talking about?" Mira asks him. "It's only been, like, a few minutes since the séance."

"What?" Jacob asks. He pulls away and looks at her like *she's* the one who's losing it. "What do you mean, *only a few minutes*?"

Again, my friends and I share a look: *What in the world is going on?*

"I mean," she says patiently, her voice suddenly soft, "the séance was only a few minutes ago." She shows her watch to Jacob. "See? The séance was midnight, and it's only twelve fifteen, and—"

"No," Jacob says, stepping backward. "No no *no*. You're in on it, too, aren't you? You're one of them."

"What are you talking about?" Rohan asks. "She's telling the truth."

"No," Jacob says. He takes another step away from us. "You're lying. I've been stuck here for days. Weeks. You don't know the things that I've seen. The things that I've had to *do*." Tears streak down his dirty face. "I saw them taken. One by one, I saw the hotel take them. I was all alone."

His next step makes him knock against an oven. The door flops open with a loud metallic bang. He doesn't seem to notice. He is completely lost in his thoughts.

"I'm alone," he mumbles on repeat. "I'm alone, I'm alone."

Seeing him like this scares me more than the

monsters. Jacob looks *broken*. If the hotel can do this . . . Chills race down my spine at the thought of the other nightmares this place could produce.

Then I realize it's not just chills from the thought.

I suddenly have the bone-deep sensation that we aren't alone.

"Jacob," I say calmly. I reach out to him like I might reach out toward a cornered animal. "Jacob, it's okay. Come with us. It's safer if you come with us."

"No!" he howls. "You're one of them! I know you're one of them!"

He turns to run.

He doesn't make it far.

"Jacob, look out!" Mira yells.

But it's too late.

We aren't alone after all.

I stumble back toward my friends as something monstrous unfolds from the oven. Black and spindly. Bones. Blackened, burnt, *cooked* bones. Dozens of them. Pouring out of the oven like an octopus, each jagged tentacle tipped in a clawed, skeletal hand.

Rohan yells in fear as the hands snap out, latching around Jacob and—in one quick movement—pulling him into the oven. The oven door slams shut behind him.

Before the three of us can run forward to help, it becomes clear that our lives are in danger, too.

Around us, the kitchen becomes terrifyingly alive.

Knives peel themselves from their blocks, hovering in the aisles, while the pots and pans hanging from the ceiling unhook and begin circling menacingly overhead, like ravenous birds. Flames burst into life on the stoves and behind the glass oven doors. The pots sitting on the burners immediately begin to boil and steam.

But the pots aren't just hissing. There are thuds within them. Thuds, and screams.

As if there are kids stuck in the pots, trying to get out.

Getting boiled alive.

Getting cooked for the hungry hotel.

If we aren't fast, we're going to be next.

18

Rohan, Mira, and I burst into motion, racing toward the far door.

The moment we move, the haunted kitchen attacks.

Butcher knives fly past us, pots and pans slam against the walls.

Mira shoves me to the side as we run, and something whizzes past my face; if she hadn't pushed me, I would have been smacked with a frying pan.

A towering stack of plates topples in front of us, crashing to the ground and exploding in shards of porcelain. We cover our faces and leap over the broken pieces.

Finally, *finally*, we make it to the door and rush out into the hall. We're going so fast we slam into the opposite wall and pause there, panting and staring as the kitchen door swings slowly shut.

Nothing comes out.

Just like before, all we're greeted with after being chased down is silence.

No banging pots,
    no crashing dishes,
        no slicing knives.

Just our frantic breathing and the heavy, empty silence of the hotel.

When the kitchen door stops swinging, Mira steps away from the wall and walks tentatively up toward it.

"Mira, don't," Rohan hisses.

She doesn't listen.

Instead, she reaches the door and pops up on tiptoes to peer in the round window.

She gasps. "No way."

"What?" I ask. I walk over and join her. When I peer through, it's easy to see why she seems shocked.

The kitchen is immaculate.

The tower of breaking dishes we leaped over is intact and resting beside the butcher block. The knives are all on their racks. The pots and pans glitter from their hooks. Everything is how we first saw it.

Impossible.

"What's going on?" Rohan asks. "Are we just imagining it all?"

"I don't think so," Mira whispers. "I mean, how would that even work?"

"A gas leak. That's how people say everyone died, isn't it?" he replies. "They say there was a gas leak and everyone just died at once. Maybe the leak is still there and it's making us hallucinate."

"This is real; it has to be," I say. "A gas leak doesn't explain the locked doors or the fact that we couldn't break the glass, or the lack of cell service."

"But that's just it," he says. "If it's all in our heads, we could be making all that up, too."

"We aren't making it up," Mira says. "If we were, how would you explain this?"

We look to her, and she holds up her arm.

There's a slice in her sleeve, and the skin beneath is glistening with blood.

"Mira, you're hurt!" Rohan gasps.

"I'm fine," she replies. "It's just a scratch. It happened when we were running. One of the knives got me."

Rohan's wide eyes look even more lost than before.

Even though she says she's okay, she doesn't look it. Before she can protest, I rip off a bit of my scarf to wrap around her arm. Because as I watch, I see that the few drops of blood falling to the carpet are getting *absorbed*.

The hotel is drinking Mira's blood.

I can practically *feel* the hotel's hunger. Its satisfaction over trapping so many of us.

I can't leave until I've found everyone.

I'm not going to leave anyone behind.

I wrap the scarf scrap tightly around Mira's arm.

"Thanks," she says.

"No problem," I reply. *I'm not going to let any harm come to you. We're going to be the last ones standing, I promise.* "Now come on—we need to get the others so we can get out of here."

"When I see Bradley again . . ." Rohan mutters as we walk down the hall.

"*If* we see Bradley again," I say. "The hotel might have already gotten him."

"Doubtful," Mira replies. "The bad ones are always taken last."

Her statement pulls me back to the hallway. The flickering light. The foreboding door. The terrible fate at the end.

The bad ones might usually be taken last. But here, I know, the good ones aren't spared, either.

19

The moment we start moving, we hear a crash at the end of the hall, and a scream that sounds less like a banshee and more like someone our age. Someone who needs our help.

"Come on," I say. We break into a run, down the long hall filled with doors and dusty painted portraits of the hotel owners.

Five steps on, and the hall lights flicker.

Go out.

Darkness swallows us.

I feel Rohan stumble and stop beside me.

"No," I say, fumbling for his arm. "Keep going!"

We keep running forward, arms outstretched so we don't crash into anything. Faintly, I can see dim green dots in the darkness. Eyes. Hundreds of pairs of eyes lining the hall. The portraits? Are the portraits staring at us with ghostly inner light?

The lights flicker back on.

The hall is no longer empty.

Skeletons stand like sentries in the doorways, still as statues. We try to skid to a halt, but we're moving too fast.

We tumble past a pair of them.

Awakening them.

One by one, their skulls snap to attention and stare at us with burning green eyes.

"Uh-oh," Rohan yelps.

Instantly the skeletons leap to attack, swiping at us with their sharp fingers, gnashing their jaws menacingly.

We duck and tumble and dodge, trying to avoid getting snatched and dragged into the darkened doorways behind the skeletal guards.

None of us want to end up like Jacob.

One of the skeletons grabs Mira's arm, but I make a fist and smash my hand as hard as I can against the skeleton's wrist. It wails out as its bones crack and splinter. It releases Mira, and the three of us run on.

The lights go out again.

This time, we're caught so off guard we stumble, collapsing to the carpet in a small pile.

"No!" Mira yells.

I close my eyes, wincing against the skeletal scratches that surely are coming, waiting for bony fingers to wrap around my neck.

But a second passes. Then another.

The lights flicker back on.

The hallway is empty. Completely empty.

Distantly, from the way we came, I swear I hear the ominous low cackle of the Grand Dame.

Laughing at our fear.

Laughing at our plight.

The three of us struggle to our feet.

"Everyone okay?" Mira asks.

"Yeah," Rohan says. He keeps looking around. "What *was* that? Where'd they go? Why didn't they take us?"

"The hotel," I say, "or whoever is in charge of the hotel, is playing with us."

"This isn't funny!" Rohan yells down the hall.

"Shh!" Mira says, nudging him in the ribs. "Don't make it mad."

"Or what?" he asks, slightly hysterical. "What could possibly be worse than this?"

"Let's not wait around to find out," I reply, and continue on toward where I hope the rest of our class is safely waiting.

20

"What are we going to do?" Rohan asks. "Even if we manage to find everyone, how are we going to get out of here?" He pauses and looks at us as we wander down the hall, heading toward the sound of the scream and wary of any more monsters or blackouts. "What do you think the hotel wants?"

"I don't know," Mira says. "But I don't think it wants us dead."

"No?" he asks. "You could have fooled me."

"Well, think about it. If this place is haunted and alive, it could take us all out whenever it wanted.

Why all the creepy monsters? Why would it let us get away?"

"Not everyone got away," I point out.

"Yes, but so far, the three of us are okay. I think . . . I think it wants to scare us. Badly. It doesn't just want us dead. It wants to play with us."

"I don't like this game," Rohan says.

"I don't, either," Mira says. "But maybe that's the key. Maybe if we refuse to be afraid, it can't hurt us."

"But why would it want us afraid in the first place?" he pushes.

Instantly, I'm transported back to the vision I had earlier.

Standing on the stage in front of the well-dressed diners.

Standing beside the Grand Dame.

Bowing. On display.

Like a sacrifice.

I stumble and nearly fall.

"Whoa," Mira says. "You okay?"

I don't know whether or not to tell her about the vision. But she felt the call to this place, too. She won't think I'm making it up. And if she believes me, Rohan will believe me, too.

"I think this is some sort of ritual," I say. "I don't know what for, or why it's happening. But I think the Grand Dame is behind it. I think she wants us to be afraid. I think she wanted us to be here so she could complete the ritual. That would explain the strange visions. And the pull you said you had toward this place."

"What are you talking about?" Rohan asks.

I hesitate. But there's no going back. Not now.

"Mira and I both felt like this place was calling to us for a long time," I say. "Did you?"

I don't look at Mira when I ask, but I have no doubt that she's ticked that I said something. But I have to know if Rohan has felt pulled into this, too.

Rohan looks between Mira and me. Finally, he replies. "No. I mean, not really."

"But you were the one who kept trying to drag me into coming along!" Mira says. "For *years*."

"Well, yeah," he says sheepishly. "But only because I thought it would be fun. You know? Spend a night in a creepy hotel. Sort of like a big scary sleepover. And then when it started to become clear that we were the unpopular kids, I thought it might help us out. But I never felt, like, pulled to be here. It's just an empty building."

"Clearly, it's not that empty," Mira says.

"But wait," Rohan says. He turns to me. "How did *you* feel the pull to come here? You just moved to town a few months ago."

Dang it.

I sigh. And decide to tell him.

"Before I moved here, I had dreams about the hotel. I didn't know they were real, or that the hotel actually existed. I just thought it was an overactive imagination. When I realized the hotel was real, well . . . I got scared. I thought I was losing my mind. But all this," I say, gesturing to the hallway, "makes me think it's something bigger. Maybe Mira and I were drawn here for a reason." I hesitate before continuing. "Maybe we were drawn here because we can defeat the Grand Dame and put all the restless souls to, well, to rest."

Mira looks at me with wide eyes.

"How would we do that?" she asks.

"Well," I say, thinking fast, "first we'd have to find the Grand Dame. And figure out her weakness."

"The only thing I want to figure out is a way out of here," Rohan interjects.

"But this might be the only way out," I tell him.

"I think the last time the ritual took place . . . I think that was the night everyone died. I think that was part of the ritual, everyone dying. Even though I have no idea what the ritual actually was *for*. Maybe she sacrificed them or something. We have to stop the Grand Dame. And if she's picking off our classmates, that means we need to protect them. And defeat her."

When I'm done talking, the silence between us is absolute. I don't know if either of them is on board. Rohan, for sure, looks like fighting the Grand Dame is the last thing he wants to do. But I *know* I'm right. I know there's a reason Mira and I felt dragged here. We have a purpose. A destiny.

"Okay," Mira finally says. "I'll do it."

"What?" Rohan protests.

She shrugs. "This hotel has already taken two people away from us, and I won't let it take any more. If the Grand Dame is behind it, she needs to be stopped. We can't just run away."

"But *how*?" Rohan asks. "I mean, this all sounds great and brave and stuff, but we're *kids*. None of us have what it takes to fight some undead evil, even if we knew what to do."

"That's why we need to find Bradley," I say. "If he

was the one who sent the email about the séance, he might know something about the Grand Dame and how to defeat her. She has to have a weakness. Everyone does."

Rohan mutters, "How do you know all of this?"

I shrug. "I didn't have a lot of friends in Florida. So I read a lot of books. They prepared me for this."

Despite everything, Rohan and Mira grin. For a brief moment, it actually feels like this might all work.

"Come on," I say, resuming our walk down the seemingly endless hall. "I swear I heard someone down here. Someone who needs our help."

Mira and Rohan nod with new conviction.

We're going to figure this out. Together.

21

We find the source of the scream at the end of the hall.

Behind an enormous wilted plant is one of our classmates. It's hard to see who it is—not only are they hiding, but there's a tattered old blanket draped over them.

I gesture for Mira and Rohan to wait, then step forward.

"Don't!" a girl's voice squeaks from under the sheet. "Don't come any closer."

"It's okay," I say. "We're friends. Classmates. We're trying to find everyone else."

"There isn't anyone else," the girl says worriedly. "They were all taken."

I'm reminded of the fear in Jacob's voice, how certain he was that he was the only one left. It makes me wonder what this girl has seen, and if she thinks she's been trapped as long as he did.

"*We* weren't taken," Mira says, stepping up beside me. "And we're stronger as a group."

"Tell that to Jacob," Rohan mutters quietly behind me. I turn around and glare at him. He just shrugs in response.

He has a point.

"It's okay," I say. "Really."

After a few more tense moments, the blanket shifts, and the girl pokes her head out.

I'm shocked. The tiny voice is coming from . . .

"Leslie?" Mira asks.

The girl nods. She no longer looks like she's strong and in charge—her shoulders are hunched, and her eyes have the same scared, lost expression as Jacob's. There's a similar worn-out look to her clothes, as though she's been here for ages, rather than just a few hours. Instead of looking at us, she peers behind Mira and Rohan and me suspiciously.

"What happened to you?" I ask. "Where did you go after the dining room?"

But Leslie only answers with another question. "Are you sure you weren't followed?"

I glance at my friends. I mean, the skeletons in the hallway didn't exactly *follow* us here, but that doesn't mean something horrible won't pop out at any moment.

"I promise," I lie.

Rohan steps forward. "I thought we'd lost you," he says. "What happened after the dining room?"

Leslie swallows hard and steps out from behind the statue, keeping the blanket wrapped around her shoulders. Like a cape. Or a shield.

"I don't know," she whispers. "I don't . . . I don't remember what happened."

"What do you mean, you don't remember?" Mira asks. Skepticism fills her voice. "One moment you were on the ceiling and the next you were gone. We thought you were taken or . . ."

"Or dead," Rohan finishes.

"I thought I was, too," Leslie whispers.

Tears fill her eyes as she stares at the three of us. She looks hopeful, like we might be able to save her.

It makes me feel kind of bad, because I don't know if that's the case. She's supposed to be the older and wiser one, here.

Once more, she doesn't answer the question. I can't tell if she's frazzled like Jacob was, or if she's outright lying.

"I thought I heard voices from in there," she says, pointing to a door down a far hall. "But I thought it was more monsters."

I sigh. "Well, we better check it out."

"No!" Leslie exclaims. "You don't know what's out there!" And she wraps herself back in the blanket, only peeking out through a tiny hole in the fabric.

Clearly, trying to wrangle everyone together so we can tackle this as a team is going to be harder than I thought. I didn't expect everyone to be so scared.

I didn't expect to be the brave one in all this.

Mira pulls me aside, back a few steps. We huddle next to Rohan.

"I don't think we can trust her," she whispers in my ear.

"What?" Rohan asks. "Why not?"

She looks to the cowering Leslie in the corner. Of everyone here, Leslie seems to be the least dangerous.

But judging from the look in Mira's eyes, she doesn't share that conviction.

"Think about it," she continues. "Leslie just *happens* to be in the hall we're in, right after we were ambushed by skeletons, right after Jacob was taken. She's the one who started this whole mess. We saw her disappear. The hotel took her. So why did it give her back?"

"Maybe she tasted funny," Rohan suggests.

Mira glares at him.

"What if she's behind it? All of it. She's leading us around and watching while everyone gets taken. What if she's being controlled by the Grand Dame somehow?"

My gut twists at the thought—not just of being controlled by the Grand Dame, but the ease with which Mira is casting blame.

"But she said the email was anonymous," Rohan says. "I thought we were convinced it was Bradley?"

She shrugs. "It could be both of them."

I look over to Leslie. She doesn't look like the type who could orchestrate something like this. She doesn't look evil. Or nefarious. Or even that brave. You'd have to be all three to try and do something like this.

"It doesn't really matter, does it?" I ask. "Even if she is behind it, we're still better off as a group. And you know what they say—keep your friends close and your enemies closer. If she's behind it all, or if she and Bradley have teamed up, the best thing we could do is keep them where we can see them. They'll have less chance of hurting us if we're all in a big group."

Mira sighs heavily. "I suppose you're right," she admits. "I just don't like the idea of having a traitor in our group."

Her words are a punch to the gut. Poor, trusting Mira. I know Leslie is just as innocent as Mira is, but it will be impossible to convince her of that.

"This time," I say, "we won't let her out of our sight." I try my best to smile at my friends. "We're in this together. Standing to the very end."

Mira and Rohan both nod. We take a step toward Leslie.

"Come on, Leslie. We're going to find the others. We'll be safer in a big group."

Leslie pokes her head out from the blanket. When she looks at us, her eyes go wide in fear.

Behind us, from the direction of the kitchen, the lights flicker.

"Oh no," Leslie whimpers. "It's her. She's back."

Leslie hides again, cowering behind the statue, as my friends and I turn to face the coming darkness. Even as fear surges through me, I feel entranced.

As the lights in the hall flicker and go out.

As the darkness becomes solid.

As two green eyes burn in the black, accompanied by red lips tilted in a sharp smile.

The Grand Dame is here.

22

A part of me wants to see her. A part of me wants to interrogate her, to ask her why she's doing this—

The rest of me knows that's stupid. She's the ghost. The monster. And she won't explain anything to me.

She just wants my classmates dead so she can complete her ritual.

She's a few hundred feet away, but she's getting closer.

With every step, the lights around her flicker
                                                    and
                                                    die.

I can't see anything more than her eyes, her lips.

But I can smell her perfume, growing stronger by the footstep. There's something intoxicating about it.

Something that makes me want to step toward her . . .

Which my body does. I see Mira moving at my side, drawing nearer to the demonic Grand Dame, too.

"What are you two doing?" Rohan yelps.

He grabs our wrists, and that knocks us from our trance. The Grand Dame is closer now. I can practically see her silhouette, a deeper black in the darkness. Too close.

We turn and flee, making sure to grab Leslie as we go. She stumbles at our side.

We run.

But the Grand Dame isn't concerned.

"I will get you, children," she coos, her voice just as entrancing as her perfume. Her words seem to hook in my bones. As if trying to draw me to her. *"There's nowhere for you to run. You are trapped here. Until my ritual is complete."*

"This way!" Rohan grunts. He pulls us down a side hallway. Lights flicker behind us.

In front of us, one of the doors is slightly ajar.

Rohan quickly opens it and gestures us inside. We rush in. Then, quiet as a mouse, he closes the door, making sure not even the latch makes a sound.

He leans against the door, his eyes squeezed shut as he listens. Silence stretches in the dimly lit bedroom. Will the Grand Dame find us in here?

I take a hesitant step forward,
    move Rohan aside,
        press my eye to the peephole,
            and wait.

I hold my breath. Seconds stretch as outside, through the fish-eye lens, the hall lights flicker.

Fade.

Darken.

Moments later, the hall is pitch-black. But somehow I can make out the shape of her.

The long black dress.

The glittering diamonds in her hair.

The Grand Dame glides down the hallway, her skin an unearthly white, like moonlight turned into flesh. Her long fingers graze the walls, the tips of her immaculate red nails leaving thin scratches in the wallpaper.

When she reaches our door, she pauses.

My heart freezes in my throat.

She turns

and looks to the door.

The breath burns in my lungs, but I don't dare let out the breath I'd been holding—it might turn into a scream.

She glides a few inches closer. So I can see every eyelash, the sharp curve of her eyeliner.

And then, she winks.

The motion makes my blood go cold.

She knows we're in here. She knows *I'm* in here.

But rather than storming forward and knocking down the door, she glides on, down the hallway.

Eventually, the hall lights flicker back on.

She's gone.

I release a huge sigh of relief.

Mira screams.

23

I nearly leap out of my skin as I turn around.

Mira and Rohan and Leslie stand side by side, eyes wide. Mira has one hand clamped to her mouth.

In the mirror, their reflections stare back.

Only, in the mirror, the reflections are smiling.

The reflections look exactly like my friends. Exactly the same, except those smiles are too big, too wicked, to fit on their faces, and their eyes are inverted: Their pupils are white, and the rest of their eyes are black as night.

"What . . . ?" I whisper.

"Don't!" Mira urges behind her hand. "Don't

come into the reflection. Or you'll be trapped."

"What do you mean?"

"I mean," Mira whispers, "we can't move. Not unless they do."

The moment she says it, the kids in the mirror take a step forward. My friends follow suit, their footsteps half a second behind, their movement clearly strained. Like reluctant puppets.

"What do I do?" I ask.

"I don't know," Mira says. She doesn't break her eyes away from the mirror. And it's then I realize that the only reason she can talk is because her mouth is hidden behind her hand. "Maybe you can break the mirror?"

In answer, Mira's reflection shakes its head. Then it moves the hand in front of its mouth down, and makes a slicing motion in front of its throat. Mira squeaks. But now that her lips are in the mirror, she can't move them.

The smile on her reflection grows wider. The message is clear:

Break the mirror and we will break your friends.

"What do you want?" I ask.

In answer, Mira, Rohan, and Leslie point their hands directly ahead, toward their reflections. They take another step forward. Only a few feet away from the mirror now; a couple more steps and they'll be touching it. I don't know what happens when they touch, but I have a horrible idea of what it might be.

I look around the room, hoping to find an answer, some sort of clue.

My friends take another step closer.

The reflections start to giggle. Their laughter is like rusted nails on glass—it makes chills shudder over my skin.

The room is a standard hotel room. On one wall is the chest of drawers with the haunted mirror. It takes up most of that wall. There's a bed on the other wall, near me, and a desk and door to the bathroom on the other side. Even if I *wanted* to break the mirror, there's nothing here to do it. Everything on this side of the room is soft, and there's no way I could run over to grab a chair. If I take two steps, I'll be in the reflection, and I'll be trapped, too.

The mirror-kids take a small, teasing step. They're close. Too close.

My friends squeal in the back of their throats, not quite screams but laced with terror.

Then Leslie takes another step forward.

The blanket she had been wearing slips off her shoulders and piles to the floor.

That's it! A blanket!

I take a hesitant step forward, trying to keep out of the mirror's grasp. Kneeling, keeping my head low, I yank the comforter off the bed. Or, at least, I try. The bed was made so perfectly and tightly that I have to tug a few times to get it loose.

When I stand, victorious, the comforter in my hands, I realize with dread that I'm already too late.

Leslie has reached the mirror, and Mira and Rohan are now closing in behind her, awaiting their turn.

Panic freezes me. Even though I'm outside the mirror's grasp, I can't move. Fear prevents it.

All I can do is watch in horror as Leslie raises her arms, as if reaching out to hug a best friend. She takes another step, Mira and Rohan in step behind her. Leslie's fingers touch the glass.

The moment they touch, the spell breaks, at least for a second.

Fast as a viper, the reflection jerks forward.

Cold, skeletal hands reach out of the mirror, grabbing Leslie's wrists. Her reflection changes, becomes monstrous—pitch-black eyes and jagged teeth and skin peeling off like bandages.

Finally, Leslie is able to scream.

Her piercing cry is enough to jolt me to action.

I toss the comforter forward, catching it on the mirror.

The comforter drapes over the mirror and the chest of drawers and Leslie's struggling shape.

Instantly, Mira and Rohan are released. They collapse in on themselves, nearly falling to their knees before catching themselves. I run forward. Not to help them, but to save Leslie. Maybe if I keep myself hidden, I can pull her away from the side.

Maybe, if—

There's a horrible shriek, then a squelching noise, like something getting sucked through gelatin.

One moment, there's a struggling form under the comforter.

Then the comforter deflates.

Falls flat against the mirror.

Goes still.

I stand there, breathing heavily beside my friends. Staring at the comforter.

"Is she . . . ?" Rohan begins. He can't complete the sentence.

"I couldn't move," I whisper. Tears form in my eyes as it becomes clear that I was too late. Too slow.

Leslie has been taken again, all because I was too cautious, too afraid.

I feel a hand on my shoulder and flinch away. But it's only Mira. She looks at me, tears in her eyes, then looks to the mirror.

"You tried," she says. She doesn't ask me to explain myself, but Rohan looks at me with a new expression in his eyes.

Not just a fear of the hotel.

A fear of me.

"I'm sorry," I say. "I was so scared. It was like I was paralyzed."

Neither of them lies—neither of them tells me it's okay.

Because it's not okay.

It's my fault.

We stand there a long time. Maybe waiting—hoping—that Leslie will come back.

None of us remove the comforter from the mirror.

She might still be back there, struggling against her reflection.

If we look, we'll be trapped, too.

If we don't look, we'll never know.

"Come on," Mira finally says. She steps up to me and takes my arm. "We can't stay in here. We need to find the others."

I nod silently.

She lets go of my arm and steps forward, looks through the peephole, and—when she deduces the coast is clear—opens the door.

"I guess she wasn't behind all this after all," Rohan says. He walks past me.

He looks at me strangely.

I know that look.

He doesn't just know it was my fault—he thinks I did it on purpose.

But he doesn't say anything. Just follows Mira out the door.

I look back once more toward the mirror, sniff loudly.

Then, before the door closes on me, I follow my friends out into the hallway.

Leslie, I know, is no more.

24

"You could have saved her," Rohan mutters under his breath as we walk slowly, cautiously down the hall. The Grand Dame is nowhere to be seen. I know she isn't here, deep in my gut. She's haunting someone else.

I can't smell her perfume.

I stop, anger flaring in my chest. I feel my cheeks flushed.

"What was that?"

"You heard me," he says sullenly. He looks at me, then down at his feet.

I draw my shoulders back, stand up to my tallest height.

"I *tried*," I say. "I already said I was sorry, okay? I was scared. I couldn't move. I—"

"Yeah, sure," he interrupts. "I'm sure that will make her parents feel a lot better when she doesn't come home. *I'm sorry, but I was too scared to save your daughter, and now she's dead.*"

My jaw drops, and Mira looks at him with shock clear in her eyes.

"Rohan!" she gasps.

"I *tried*," I repeat, my voice becoming a growl. *How dare he?* "I didn't see *you* doing anything."

"I was stuck. Like, really stuck. Unlike you. Who could have done something."

"What are you saying?" I ask. Because I know what he's saying, but I want to hear him say it aloud.

"I'm saying, I think maybe you *wanted* her to get taken."

"I can't believe this," Mira says.

"I can't, either," Rohan says. "I can't believe we trusted her."

"No," Mira interjects. I can't speak—my breath is hot, and I know if I say something, I'll regret it later. I can't push Rohan away. I need him to stay with us. We can't lose the group.

Mira goes on, "I can't believe you'd say that. She saved your life, Rohan! Back in the dining room. If she hadn't been there, holding on, we'd both be gone. She could have let us go, but she held on. She saved us. She saved *you*."

Rohan doesn't say anything. Instead, he takes a big, deep breath and stares at Mira's shoes.

"The hotel is playing with our minds," Mira continues. "It's getting under our skin. Bringing out the worst in us. We can't let it tear us apart. We can't let it win. Right, Jasmine?"

I nod. I still don't trust myself to say anything.

"Come on," Mira says. "Jasmine tried. And she's right. We need to find the group. We need to find Bradley and find a way out of here, and we're only going to do that as a team. We're only going to do it if we trust one another."

Rohan mutters something, but I can't hear it.

That's probably for the best.

"Fine," he says, a little louder. He shakes himself, as if trying to get rid of a bad thought. "You're probably right. I'm tired. And hungry." He pauses and finally looks up, giving me a sheepish smile. "And I lost my hot chocolate a few hours ago."

Despite everything, I exhale a laugh, the anger and fear fading.

I didn't push him away. He may be a jerk, but we haven't lost him.

"Sorry," he says.

"It's okay," I reply. "This place is a nightmare, and Mira's right: We have to trust one another."

He nods.

But as he turns and we continue down the hall, searching for the rest of our class, I can tell he doesn't trust me. Not one bit. I just try to tell myself that it doesn't matter.

So long as we make it to the end, it doesn't matter if he trusts me or not.

25

We wander the halls for the next half hour. We poke through every open door, peering into storage cupboards and abandoned service hallways and tiny alcoves that hold ice machines. But we don't find any stragglers. When we reach the doors leading to the pool—even from outside, I can smell the faint chlorine and eucalyptus scents—my watch says it's nearly three.

Mira covers a yawn with the back of her hand as we pause outside the doors. I put my ear to the wood.

My eyes widen.

"I hear them," I whisper.

Victory whirls in my chest. They're here! We found them!

Slowly, carefully—in case it's a trap—I push the door open a crack and look inside.

At first, I don't see anyone. Just the empty pool chairs still draped with frayed and moth-eaten towels lining the pool. But the voices are louder. I open the door a bit more and poke my head in.

Our entire class—what's left of them, at least—is huddled together in the deep end of the empty pool, circled around a few small lanterns like they're huddled around a fire. Even though the rest of the hotel is brightly lit and warm, it's dark and cold in here. It makes me wonder if the lights aren't working, or if the kids turned the lights off.

I push the door a bit more, and the loud squeak announces my arrival.

Everyone's face jerks toward me, eyes wide and fearful.

I almost laugh—they look like scared little mice, cowering together with their hands to their chests—but I force it down. Mira and Rohan step in beside me, and as they do, one of the kids in the huddle steps forward.

Bradley.

"Who is it?" he calls out.

"Mira," Mira replies. "And Rohan. And Jasmine."

Bradley grunts. Clearly, he's not happy to see us. Which is just fine. Normally, I wouldn't be happy to see him, either, but I'm honestly a little grateful he's here.

Like Mira said—we're safer in a group.

"How do we know you're real?" Bradley asks.

It's then I realize he isn't just standing there—he has something in his hands. It looks like a crowbar.

"Because we all think you're a jerk," Rohan blurts out. "Proof enough for you?"

Someone snickers. Bradley glares back at his friend Bo, who quickly puts a hand over his mouth. Chet is nowhere to be seen.

When it's clear they aren't going to attack, we step farther into the room.

"What are you doing in there?" I ask when we near the pool's edge.

"Felt safer," Bradley replies. Apparently, he's appointed himself the group leader. Why am I not surprised? "Too many windows, and from here we can see every entrance."

I raise an eyebrow, but don't push it. I'd have thought the dining rooms or even the indoor tennis court would feel safer, but whatever—I'm clearly not in charge.

"Is this everyone?" I ask. I don't get into the pool. Neither do Rohan and Mira.

"Everyone we could find," he says. "We went out in teams to look for any stragglers. This is all that was left."

He takes a few steps forward so he doesn't have to shout toward us. I kind of like being up here while he's down there—for once, he's not looking down on *me*. It's nice to have the roles reversed.

His eyebrows narrow. "I'm surprised no one found you."

I shrug. "We were looking for you guys. Maybe we just kept missing one another. I mean, don't they say if you want to get found, you should just stay in one place?"

"Where's Leslie?" he asks.

My feeling of being above him goes away.

"We lost her," Mira says softly. Bradley clearly looks like he's about to say something cutting, and she continues: "Where's Chet?"

Bradley's open mouth snaps shut. He bites his lip before answer.

"We lost him," he replies.

Silence stretches between us for a while.

"So," Rohan says. "What's the plan?"

Bradley gestures back to the group of kids. "That's what we were trying to figure out," he says. "We don't know."

"I find that hard to believe," I say.

He narrows his eyes.

"What are you talking about?"

"You know what I'm talking about," I say, looking down at him, trying to pull back some confidence. I raise my voice so everyone in the pool can hear me. "After all, you're the one who planned all this."

He gasps in shock, his eyes going wide.

"We know what you did," I continue, before I lose confidence. Before he can defend himself.

"And what did I do?"

I persist. "You're the one who sent Leslie the email about the séance, weren't you?"

A few of the kids huddled in the pool step closer to us. They glance at one another nervously.

"What?" He looks at me like I've lost my mind. "Why would you even think that?"

"Oh come on, stop pretending," I say. "You're the biggest jerk in school, and all you've talked about this last month is how scared we were all going to be. How this was going to be the scariest year yet. You *knew* about the séance. And how else would you know, unless you were the one telling Leslie all about it?"

He just glares at me, anger simmering beneath the surface, so I continue.

"And if you knew about the séance, that means you knew about the Grand Dame, and the ritual, and what the séance would do. And if you know about her, you probably know how to defeat her, don't you? You know how to get out. You're just waiting around, biding your time, letting everyone get picked off one by one so you can walk out of here the bravest kid in Gold River."

I'm practically panting when I'm done talking. There's a fierce, hot anger in my chest. At Bradley, for making fun of me and everyone else. At the kids from my old school, for always treating me like a reject. At the hotel, for nearly turning my friends on me. Mira puts a hand on my arm, but I don't know if it's to tell me it's okay or to calm me down so I don't freak out again.

I fully expect Bradley to bow his head in defeat, or to look ashamed for what he's done.

He doesn't.

Instead, he starts to shake his head, an incredulous smile growing on his face.

He doesn't look defeated in the slightest. In fact, he looks even more like an empowered bully.

"Are you done?" he asks.

I don't say anything or move a muscle. I just stare at him, my friends at my side.

"It's funny you should say all that," Bradley says. "Because we were just agreeing the same thing about *you*."

26

Now it's my turn to step back in shock.

"What?"

His smile grows. "Yeah. I mean, it makes sense. Kids have been doing this dare for years, and no one's ever gotten hurt. *Ever.* Sure, they get scared off, but it's just nerves, or some upperclassman playing a joke. No one *actually* sees any ghosts in here. Even Leslie's performance earlier was just that—a performance. You know how those theater kids like to be the center of attention and make up stories."

The others gather around him now, and I start to feel like I'm falling as his accusation presses on.

"So then here comes along a new girl, little Miss Jasmine, and no one knows anything about her except she says she's from Florida. No one sees her dad, and her mom is long gone, and the year she shows up, the hotel comes to life and starts hurting people. *You're* the only new thing here, Jasmine. *You're* the only possible reason the hotel would be coming to life."

"But the anniversary," Mira interjects. I'm grateful she's standing up for me, but even her argument seems weak. "The séance."

"Yeah," he continues. "And who else would have the most to gain by telling Leslie about it? Think about it—I'm already the most popular kid in school. I don't *need* to last the night here. I don't even need to be here! Next year, I'll still be popular. The only one who needs the popularity boost is Jasmine. And her dopey friends."

Rohan steps forward. I fully expect him to come to my rescue—after all, no one hates Bradley more than he does.

"I hate to say it," he tells me, "but Bradley has a point."

My gut drops to my feet.

"What?" Mira and I gasp at the same time. Her hand tightens on my arm.

Rohan doesn't look at us. Or at Bradley. He doesn't look anyone in the eye as he talks.

"You admitted it yourself," he says. "You'd felt a pull to this place before you even got into town. And you were so quick to want to come here."

"Because you pressured me!" I yelp.

He swallows. And doesn't say another word.

"See?" Bradley says. "Not even your own *friend* believes you're innocent. Just admit it, Jasmine. This was all your fault. *You* sent Leslie the séance. *You* planned the whole thing. You wanted to become popular in a school where no one likes or even knows you, and this was your pathetic attempt at becoming the center of attention."

"That's not it at all," I say, panic and anger racing in my veins.

I've never said a truer statement in my life.

"Stop lying," Bradley says. "You knew about the Grand Dame. And the ritual. You're just trying to point blame at me because it's easy and you don't want others to hate you. Well, too late. We're getting out of here, Jasmine. It's almost sunrise, and soon our parents will come looking for us, and we'll be free. But you'll go to jail."

My thoughts burn as fast as a wildfire. This wasn't how this was supposed to go down. People weren't supposed to be siding with Bradley. How could they? How could they think I would ever do this?

I open my mouth, struggling to find words to defend myself.

Before I can speak, a horrible cackle fills the room, echoing in the hollow space, coming from everywhere and nowhere all at once. Along with the telltale scent of perfume.

The Grand Dame has found us.

27

"*Silly little children,*" the Grand Dame sneers. "*Squabbling amongst yourselves, when the real danger is still near.*"

"Run!" someone yells.

"Where?" another kid responds.

The Grand Dame's voice floats around the room, circling in the shadows. She could be anywhere.

I know she is everywhere.

The shadows at the edges of the room darken. Congeal. Become a thick, heavy tar that drips down the walls and over the floor. A sludge that pushes against the abandoned lounge chairs, scraping their metal legs against the concrete.

The kids in the pool scramble for the exits, but the sludge around the pool is as fast as it is thick. It spills over the edges of the pool, down the far steps, making it impossible to get out—I watch as kids slip and slide, trying to escape but unable to get a strong hold.

"Hurry!" Rohan yells. He and Mira rush to the edge of the pool. Our end, miraculously, isn't covered in sludge, but that clearly won't be the case for long. It's already seeping toward us, cutting off escape to either side. The only way out is behind us, back into the hall.

A few of the kids start to run over, but then a terrible gurgling noise comes from the drains in the pool.

The sludge

  bubbles

    up.

The thick black grime slurps out of the drains, achingly fast. It curls around the kids' feet, snares them in place, or else causes them to slip and slide to their knees. Instantly, everyone in the pool is covered in black muck that rises by the second. The room is a deafening mix of screams and slurps and the Grand Dame's triumphant cackles. Mira and Rohan desperately try to pull kids up from the sludge as it rises past their waists. But their hands are slick, and no one can get out.

Not even Bradley.

He vainly scrambles up the pool wall in front of me. His normally cruel eyes are wide with fear as his oiled fingers try again and again to grab hold of the slick ledge. Rohan and Mira are crying as the sludge nears us. They reach out for the hands of the trapped kids, but no one can gain a firm grip.

In seconds, the pool will be filled.

In seconds, the sludge will surround and consume Mira and Rohan and me, too.

I kneel down.

"Help me!" Bradley calls out.

I reach out my hand.

I'm not a monster.

I'll prove to them I'm not a monster.

Bradley's hand clamps around mine. I steady myself against the edge of the pool. Our grip is strong. But his palm is sweaty, and he weighs more than me, and the sludge rises past his chest, a heavy, living thing, and I can't pull him out.

I strain.

I pull with all my might.

"Get me out!" Bradley calls. His other hand grasps for the ledge, but it's covered in sludge and he can't help pull himself free.

"I'm trying!" I yell back.

From the corners of my eyes, I see Mira and Rohan struggling to pull out two other kids.

Farther on, the sludge rises to my classmates' necks. Sucking them down.

Devouring them.

Rohan looks over to me. Panic is clear in his eyes, and I hope he sees the panic in mine.

"We have to—" I call.

But I don't finish the sentence.

With a sickening *slurp*, the girl in Rohan's hands is yanked away. Sucked under. The poor girl only has time for one quick squeak before she disappears completely under the black.

Rohan falls back to his butt and then scrambles to his feet.

Coming to help.

I look down at Bradley.

"Please," Bradley says. "Please help. I didn't mean it. I didn't—"

The sludge yanks him.

Our grips slip.

Bradley's eyes widen in fear. In recognition.

Just as Rohan comes to help me, Bradley is pulled under the blackness. Never to be seen again.

28

"I tried," I say desperately. I scramble back toward the edge of the pool, but there's no seeing through the sludge. Bradley is gone. "He just—he just—"

"Come on!" Rohan yells. He grabs my arm and pulls me back.

As the sludge boils up and spills over the edge of the pool. As it seeps toward our feet.

He drags me over to Mira, who's struggling with another kid. The moment we near, the boy is yanked out of her hands with a squelching slurp, and Mira stumbles back, into Rohan's arms. Tears stream down her face.

"I have to help him!" she calls.

But even she knows there's no point. We take a fumbling step backward, looking out at the pool. Thick black sludge fills it to the brim, spills over, blends with the oil dripping down the walls, turning the whole room into a roiling miasma of black. Our classmates have all been consumed by the darkness. There isn't a trace of them, not even bubbles of breath.

If we aren't quick, we're going to join them.

I glance behind me. The path to the pool doors is still clear, but the oil is edging in, narrowing our escape.

"We have to go," I say. "Quickly! Run! If it touches you, we're done for!"

Still crying, Mira stumbles forward, Rohan helping at her side. They race ahead of me, and I'm close behind.

When they are past the door, I pause.

Turn around as chills race up my spine.

To see the Grand Dame rising from the sludge in the center of the pool, her black dress glistening like an oil slick, her red smile like a cut.

She nods her head. As if thankful.

I turn and run through the door to rejoin my friends.

29

We collapse in a heap against the far wall, panting and fearful. But only for a moment.

"Come on," I say, gasping for breath. I force myself to stand. "We have to keep moving."

"But they're . . . they're . . ." Mira stammers.

"They're gone," I say. "We tried. There's nothing we can do for them anymore. We can only try to save ourselves. Please. We have to move."

As if to accentuate my point, the pool doors in front of us bulge slightly.

Oil begins to puddle out from beneath, glinting in the warm light of the hallway.

I swear, as I look into its smooth, reflective surface, that I'm able to see my classmates, calling out, trapped in some dark netherworld.

I look away and pull Mira to her feet. Rohan is already upright.

"Where do we go?" he asks. "Where's safe?"

Nowhere, I want to say, but that's not what they need to hear.

I rack my brain.

My dreams come back into focus.

> Walking down the flickering hallway.
>
> Toward the door that I know leads to death.

Why, when I think of it now, does it feel like the only way forward?

"We'll find something," I try to reassure Rohan.

He clearly doesn't believe me, but as the oil keeps pouring in, he doesn't fight. Taking Mira's hand, he starts jogging down the hall. I follow at his side.

"We tried to save them, right?" Mira pants.

"Yes," I say. "We tried. There was nothing we could have done."

Rohan shoots me a look. I can't tell what he's thinking, but I know it isn't good.

Finally, we stumble out into the main lobby.

There's absolutely no trace that we were here before. The candles and fire pit and toppled statues are all gone. Instead, the lobby is immaculate, looking exactly like it would have thirty-three years ago. Plush armchairs and chaise lounges are arranged around thriving tropical plants and glowing lamps. Crystal champagne flutes are in a neat circle on a pedestal by the entryway, and bubbles rise and fizz in the filled glasses. A small buffet table is set up with breads and fruits and cheeses.

"Does anyone else get the feeling that we're arriving for a party?" Rohan asks.

I don't answer. Instead, I walk over and collapse on a chaise. Mira sits down next to me. But she keeps looking around, clearly waiting for the nightmare to resume.

"What are we going to do?" she asks. "Can we save them?"

I swallow.

"I don't know," I say, even though I feel there's no way to save them. Not now. The hotel has them. Just as it has us. Just as it has the three hundred people who died here.

And it's not letting any of us go. Not until it gets what it wants: all of us.

Rohan paces back and forth in front of us.

I glance over to the table with food. My stomach rumbles, but I'm not about to eat. With our luck, the food is probably all poisoned.

"We have to figure out a way out of here," Rohan says. "There has to be a way. And when we get out, we can find a way to save our classmates."

"Rohan—"

"No!" he says, turning on Mira. "We can't give up right now. We're so close. It's almost dawn. You heard what Bradley said—once the sun rises, our parents will look for us and they'll know to look here. Heck, most of *them* did the Dare when they were kids. They'd know we're here."

I shake my head.

"That's not going to work," I say. "If we wait for them, it will be just like thirty-three years ago. The hotel is only going to let someone new in if everyone inside is already dead."

"And how would *you* know?" Rohan says. He takes a step forward.

"Rohan . . ." Mira says again, this time in a tone that clearly says *don't push it*.

"What? You heard Bradley. He has a point. Jasmine has more to gain from all this than he did. And he's . . . gone. He wouldn't have done this. And Jasmine says she's seen this place before. That she felt pulled toward this place. She—"

"We both did!" Mira yells. "Haven't you been listening? We've both felt pulled in by this place. It's not just her."

Rohan just shakes his head.

"How could I have trusted either of you? How could I have let you convince me to come here?"

"*What?*" I can't believe what I'm hearing. "You *begged* us to come here, Rohan. You wouldn't shut up about it. How dare you accuse us of—"

"Yeah, but I wouldn't have invited you along if I'd known you were going to do all this," he says, his voice and arms raised. "You trapped us here. You killed everyone."

"They aren't dead," I say. "At least, I don't think so." *At least, not yet. Not until the Grand Dame has done her ritual.*

"There's still hope," Mira says.

"No," Rohan replies. "I'm not doing this anymore. Not with you two. I'm getting out of here, but I'm doing it on my own."

He turns and starts walking away, toward the entrance, as though the doors will magically just open up for him. Mira rises, but I reach out and stop her.

"Don't," I say softly. "Just let him go. He'll come back around."

Mira looks between me and Rohan, torn. But she is clearly hurt from Rohan's accusation, too. She sits back down, defeated, as Rohan reaches the door.

He immediately starts pounding on it.

"Let us out!" he yells. "Do you hear me? Let! Us! Out!"

"Why don't you just try the handle?" I say sarcastically.

He looks back at me, shoots me a glare.

Then he reaches down and grabs the handle.

"Gee, like this?" he growls.

And yanks open the door.

30

For a moment, for one
> terrible,
> hopeful
> moment, we all stare at the
open door in shocked amazement. Cold air whips
through, making the champagne flutes rattle.

It also sends a curious buzzing through my head,
through my whole body, like an electric charge ramp-
ing up to ten, as deeper in the hotel, a grandfather
clock begins to clang.

We look toward a clock in the lobby. 3:33.

Things click.

Somehow I know this was when the ritual took place.

3:33.

"What—" he whispers.

He doesn't get to finish his question.

Because as the bell tolls, shapes come out of the shadows.

Not monsters.

Hotel guests.

The buzzing inside my head grows louder. My hands clench on the arm of the chaise and on Mira's hand. She yelps in pain, but it takes all my concentration to keep from screaming as the buzzing grows, becomes a tremor that shakes my bones.

As ghostly guests fill the hall, all dressed in their evening wear.

As they pick up champagne flutes or peruse the table of hors d'oeuvres.

As one of them picks up Rohan as if he weighs nothing and carries him away from the door.

As the ghosts crowd us, preventing us from moving, preventing us from getting to Rohan.

As the shaking inside me gets so strong, my teeth rattle.

As the Grand Dame appears in the center of the room, a wicked smile on her face, and looks directly at me.

I can't fight it anymore.

The buzzing and the tremors take over, and I crash into another vision.

31

"*Come,*" the Grand Dame says. "*The time is at hand. Bring her forward.*"

The cloth bag is removed from my head, and darkness explodes into flickering light.

It takes a while for me to blink away the stars, to make sense of where I am. It's not the lobby, and it's not the dining room like I saw in the previous vision.

No, I'm somewhere that makes my bones shake and acidic fear pulse in my veins.

I'm in the basement. This, I know, is the room where my dreams had been taking me. This is the room that ends in death.

Concrete walls surround me, and three hundred hotel guests crowd in the cramped space. All of them are wearing their finest evening wear, and all of them wear black silk masks, hiding their features. But not hiding their expectant, eager smiles.

Someone shoves me forward, and I stumble into the center of the cleared space.

The Grand Dame stands there, somehow even more imposing than before. She alone isn't wearing a mask. She doesn't need to hide her face.

She's proud of what she's doing. Of what she's achieved so far.

She holds out a hand, and some force overtakes me. I reach out and step toward her, letting her fingers grasp coldly around mine. I don't fight. I don't think I could if I tried.

She has me totally under her control.

"Tonight, my friends," the Grand Dame says, *"we finally complete our life's work. You, who have gathered from near and far. You, who have helped find this perfect location—a confluence of energy lines, the perfect cosmic axis. The one place where the veil between the worlds is thinnest. You, who have worked so hard. Now our work has paid off. Tonight, the communing is at hand. Tonight, we do what no living mortal has done before."*

A ripple moves through the crowd, a murmur of excitement.

"*Tonight,*" she says, "*we open the doors between the worlds of the living and the dead. We become the masters of death, and thus of life itself!*"

She cackles with glee, sending chills down my spine. The rest of the group laughs and cheers as well.

Only I stand silent. My mouth magically sealed shut.

I shouldn't be here.

Not in this basement, with its walls and floors covered in strange symbols.

Not with these people, with their strange clothes and scary masks.

Not with this woman, who said she would take me home when she saw me outside school.

Memories jumble. Suddenly, I am fully inside of Sarah's head. Suddenly, I no longer remember being Jasmine—just this scared little girl from thirty-three years ago.

The Grand Dame was the mayor's wife. I'd known her all my life. She had organized so many charity functions, had set up the local orphanage, had even single-handedly funded the building of the Carlisle Hotel. All—she said—so Gold River could flourish.

She was trusted and loved by everyone. Rebecca was her name. But here, they only refer to her as the Grand Dame.

How was I supposed to know it was a trick? A trap?

How was I supposed to know she was evil?

The Grand Dame slices her hand through the air. Laughter cuts off sharply.

"*Enough,*" she says. "*The time is now. Link hands, my friends. The stars align. The ritual begins.*"

Around me, the hotel guests all clasp hands.

The Grand Dame begins speaking, but it's not in any language I understand. It's deep, guttural, like it's made of earth and clay and electricity. Her words rumble through the room, and the rest of the guests pick up the sound.

Energy hums through my veins.

It feels wrong. So wrong.

Symbols on the wall and floor begin to glow, a sickly, neon green light that writhes and slithers. Like poison.

I can't move. The Grand Dame's hands are on my shoulders, and fear or magic root me in place.

As the lights flare in the floor.

As the power grows.

All I can think is: *I don't want to be here. I want to be home.*

As the light fills me, all I see are my parents' loving faces. I miss them. I want them to be here. To save me. To help me.

"*No,*" I hear through the chanting. "*No, this isn't right. Something is wrong. Something—*"

And then, the Grand Dame starts to scream.

The green light fills me. Vibrates in my bones.

The light is unhappy.

The light wants revenge.

I just want to go home. I just want to go home. Help me, Mom and Dad. Help me.

32

"Help me, Jasmine," Mira says. "You have to wake up! You have to help me!"

The room swims sluggishly into focus as the vision fades and drips away. Green light is replaced by warm candelabras and fireplaces. The chanting, worried faces of the guests and the Grand Dame are replaced by Mira's frantic gaze.

"We have to move, please wake up, they have him, they have him." Her words are so fast I can barely make them out. Finally, sense returns to me. I realize we're in the lobby. Back in the lobby, in the present day.

And we are alone.

I push myself up to sitting—how did I end up on the floor?—and rub the back of my head. My eyes ache, and my head throbs, and every inch of me feels like it was hit with a meat tenderizer.

"What happened?" I manage. Just talking makes my head throb.

"They took him," Mira says. Tears run down her cheeks. She keeps looking over her shoulder, toward the halls. "You started shaking and screaming and then they took him and I was so scared I didn't know what to do."

Memories rush back. Not only the vision, but of the lobby filling with the ghostly guests. One of them grabbing Rohan.

I shiver with a sudden cold. But it isn't fear. At least, not *just* fear.

When I look to the hotel entrance, I see that the door is still open.

I gasp.

"Mira," I say.

"What?" She doesn't look away from deeper in the lobby, where they took Rohan.

"Mira, the door. Look!"

She does. Her eyes widen.

"Is this a trap?" she asks.

"I don't think so," I reply. "I mean, the ghosts are all gone. They're all in the basement."

"How do you know?" she asks. There's the slightest note of suspicion in her voice.

No. She has to believe me. If this is going to work, she has to trust me.

"I had a vision," I say. "I think they went to the basement."

Slowly, carefully, I stand. I wobble slightly; the room swims.

I turn to the open door. Snow drifts inside. It doesn't melt when it hits the cold carpet.

"We could leave," I say. The words trip from my mouth before I can stop them. "Go and get help. Find some adults. The police. Someone else."

Mira looks at the door. I can see the battle raging behind her eyes.

"What can the two of us do to save him?" I ask. "To save any of them? We're in over our heads," I say. "Maybe adults could help?"

For a moment, I think she'll agree with me. She stares at the door for a few tense breaths. Then she looks at me.

"You say you've always felt pulled to this place?" she asks.

I swallow and nod solemnly.

"And so have I," she says. "I think that means . . . I think that means it's up to us to stop it. Adults won't be able to save Rohan. Only us."

"But we could *die*," I say. I can't quite believe what she's saying.

"I know," she says. She takes my hand. "But we're meant to do this. We're meant to end it. Together."

I take a deep breath. I look to the open door.

The last chance to back out.

The last chance to leave this all behind.

Then I look to her and nod.

"Okay," I say. "Let's save him."

And, hand in hand, we turn from the open door and walk back. Deeper into the hotel.

To where the nightmare began.

33

"How do we get to the basement?" she asks when we've left the lobby.

We stand at a crossroads—identical hallways stretch out in three directions.

Now that we stand here, the silence is a heavy emptiness that presses down on my shoulders.

It's more than a hunger.

It's a void.

A wound.

Thirty-three years ago, something went terribly wrong in this hotel, and it's been suffering ever since.

I look to Mira.

I know where to go.

"Do you trust me?" I ask her.

She doesn't hesitate, even though I fully expect her to.

"Of course," she replies.

"Then I know where to go," I say. "I think the hallway in my dreams was a clue. I think it leads to the basement. Where they took him." I pause. "Are you sure you want to do this? There's no going back if you say yes."

She hesitates.

"If it will save him, and everyone else, then yes. We were pulled here for a reason. I'm not leaving until I know what it is."

"Okay, then," I say. "Let's go."

I swallow a dozen different emotions and turn, heading down one of the halls, following my gut. My feet guide me, moving of their own accord.

"What happened to you in there?" Mira asks as we walk. Her voice is barely above a whisper. "In the vision?"

I look at her. "You really want to know?"

She nods.

"I saw . . . I saw this place as it was thirty-three years ago. Like I was there. They were—the Grand

Dame and all the hotel guests—they were sacrificing this girl, I think. Sarah." I still don't tell her that *I* was in the body of the girl about to be sacrificed. That would freak her out too much. "They said it would 'open the door between the worlds' or something. They said they would be able to control life and death." I swallow. "But it went wrong. I . . . I don't know what happened. But it didn't go to plan."

Mira nods, taking all of this in stride. As if it's perfectly rational and logical. And I guess, after everything we've gone through tonight, it sort of is.

"And now they're trying to complete the ritual," she finishes.

"Yeah," I say.

"And I bet that's why they took Rohan down here. They're going to sacrifice him."

I pause outside a plain door. One that looks like it would lead to a service closet or something.

"Yeah," I reply. "I think you're right."

"Then we definitely have to do this," she says. "I won't let anyone hurt him. Or you. And hopefully there's a way to get everyone else out as well."

I look at her and smile. My hand reaches toward the doorknob.

"You're the most selfless person I've ever met," I say.

"I hear that a lot," she replies, joking.

I open the door.

Concrete stairs lead down. Lit by a flickering, cold bulb.

"All right, then," I say. "Let's end this."

34

It's one thing to dream of a place. To dream of walking toward doom, that sense of foreboding.

It's another to actually be living it.

My body shakes as we make our way down the steps. Mira puts a hand on my shoulder as she trails behind me.

"There's nothing to be scared of," she says.

I don't know how she can be so calm after everything she's seen. I don't know how she can be so brave that she's able to comfort me.

Maybe she truly is that selfless. In hoping to save Rohan, she's able to cast away all fear. It's impressive.

"I'm okay," I say. But her comfort doesn't stop my shaking. My veins fill with a similar electricity as before. A fear. An anticipation.

An excitement.

The stairs lead down.

Down.

Down at least three stories, until we are so deep within the earth I can practically feel the ground beyond the concrete walls pressing in, can practically feel it breathing. Flickering neon lights illuminate our descent, casting sharp shadows on the walls and floor as we walk.

Our shadows look like ghosts.

Phantoms.

The light is otherworldly. Makes me feel like I'm not really there.

Like we've already lost.

Like we're already dead.

That, and with every step, the cold electricity grows in my bones.

The tug in my chest tightens, strengthens. Pulls me forward.

We reach the hall.

It is exactly like in my dreams.

Every crack.

Every loose pebble.

Every shadow.

I hold back a gasp and fight down the adrenaline that courses through my veins. This is it.

This is it.

I know what waits behind that door.

Death.

Death.

No matter if I open it in my dreams or in real life, the only thing behind that door is death.

"Are you okay?" Mira asks softly.

I nod.

"It's exactly like in my dreams," I say. I swallow. "Except . . . this is the part where I always woke up."

She smiles at me sadly, resolve deep in her eyes.

"Well, we aren't waking up," she says. "So let's end this nightmare once and for all. It's time to get everyone back."

She reaches out and takes the doorknob.

Then, before either of us can change our minds, she opens the door, and we step inside the pitch-black room.

35

"Don't!" Rohan yells the moment we step into the room. "It's a trap!"

It's too late.

The door slams behind us, and lights flare into being.

Dozens of candles and torches and lanterns are scattered throughout the room. All of them held in ghostly hands. The room is thick with ghosts—three hundred of them. All of them are wearing their formal evening wear, just like their final moments down here. All of them wear masks. Except now, their faces are gaunt and skeletal, their skin pulled tight, cheeks caved in and hands gnarled and bony.

All of them, except for the Grand Dame.

She stands in the center of the room, regal as ever, in her long black velvet dress with its fur collar. Her hair cascades down her shoulders, diamonds glittering in the firelight. Her green eyes snare Mira and me to the ground.

Just as she has Rohan snared in front of her.

Rohan's arms and legs are tied tight, and the Grand Dame's hand is over his mouth.

"*Indeed,*" the Grand Dame says. "*It was a trap. And you walked into it so willingly.*"

I glance over to Mira. I expect her to cower in the face of the Grand Dame. The Grand Dame, who radiates so much power and strength. Who, even now, when half-dead and half-alive, seems so much stronger, so much *bigger*, than Mira and me combined.

But Mira just glares at the Grand Dame.

Mira pulls herself up taller.

"I'm not going to let you hurt him," she says. "Or anyone else. Not anymore."

"*Oh?*" the Grand Dame replies. She squeezes Rohan's shoulder with her free hand. He squeaks in pain. "*Are you so sure?*"

Mira swallows and looks at me for backup. I just look at her, wide-eyed, frozen. Now that I'm here, I can't actually believe this is happening.

I know what is about to occur. And I can't bring myself to believe that, either.

"*Take them,*" the Grand Dame says.

Instantly, a few ghosts break away from the crowd and grab Mira and me, pulling us apart. It's only then that I realize we were still holding hands. We struggle against our captors, but it's no use. Even though they're ghosts, their grips are strong as steel.

"*Now,*" the Grand Dame says, "*I believe we had a ritual to finish. Wouldn't you agree?*"

"I know what you're doing," Mira says. "But it won't work. It failed before, and it will fail again. You can't just go sacrificing kids so you can talk to the dead."

The Grand Dame laughs.

"*Is that what you think we're doing?*" The Grand Dame smiles. "*My dear, stupid girl. I didn't spend years* researching ley lines and astrological formulae, and millions of dollars building this hotel in the perfect location, just so I could talk to the dead! That's ridiculous. Why, we're here to control life and death itself. When I successfully complete this ritual, I will be immortal."

"What about the others?" Mira asks. She gestures to the ghosts with her head. "Won't they get immortality, too?"

The Grand Dame smiles. "Of course not, dear. They're already dead. A tragic accident, as I'm sure you'll agree. But! So long as the hotel stands, they can stay here for free. A different sort of eternal life, perhaps. And one with fantastic hospitality."

She cackles at her own joke.

"What about our classmates?" I ask. "Are they dead?"

"Not yet," the Grand Dame says. "The hotel needs feeding, after all. Consider them in the storage cupboard. Kept aside until they're needed."

Her smile goes sharp.

"Now, enough talk. The time is nigh. The planets align. And now, thirty-three years later, we have the perfect sacrifice. This time, the ritual will work. And I will live forever!"

The Grand Dame squeezes Rohan's shoulder tighter, and he screams out, muffled behind her hand.

Mira's scream is louder.

"No!" Mira says. "Please. Don't hurt him. Don't hurt either of them. If you'll let them go, all of them, you can . . ." She swallows. "You can take me."

The Grand Dame's eyes narrow.

Hope flutters in my chest.

"You are willing to sacrifice yourself to save your friends?"

Mira looks at me. There are tears brimming, but she doesn't cry. She looks to the Grand Dame and nods.

"Yes," Mira says. "I'll sacrifice myself if it means saving their lives."

The Grand Dame smiles.

"A pure sacrifice," she says. *"One without fear or regret or attachment. How selfless of you. Do you swear you give yourself freely, in place of your friend here, no matter the cost?"*

Light flickers around the Grand Dame as she asks it, cold and wicked green, the same as her eyes.

"I do," Mira says. "If you let him go, I'll do it. I'll do anything."

That same green light twines around Mira's throat and chest. As if binding her to her word.

Laughter fills the room.

But it's not the Grand Dame's.

It's mine.

36

Bradley was wrong about so many things.

He thought he had it all figured out. Thought being the bully meant no one could touch him. He thought he was the meanest kid. Unstoppable.

Wrong. Wrong. Wrong.

But he was right about one thing:

I *am* a monster.

But it's not my fault.

Kids like him made me this way. It's what they wanted me to be. I can't help it that I listened.

The Grand Dame gestures at the ghosts holding me, and they let me go.

Mira's determination is replaced with confusion.

I can't stop laughing. Not only from the expression on her face, but from how well this worked out. How *easy* it was.

"Jasmine?" Mira asks. "Jasmine, what's going on?"

I look to the Grand Dame. I know we don't have much time—only a few more minutes before the planetary alignment is off—but she gestures at me to continue.

I've waited so long to tell *someone*.

"I lied," I say simply. Smugly. A big smile on my face as her own face falls.

"What?"

"Yeah," I reply. "Rohan was right all along. So was Bradley. The séance was my idea. I emailed Leslie. I can't believe she fell for it so easily. I can't believe you *all* fell for it so easily."

"I don't understand," she gasps. "Why?"

Anger burns in my chest. I remember the laughter of the kids in my old school. Laughing because I was different. Laughing because my mom had died, the most terrible laughter of all.

"Because this is my one chance to get my mother back," I say. "Remember how I told you that I had dreams of this place? And visions? Visions of a ritual, and a girl being sacrificed? Well, that girl—Sarah—that was my *mom*."

Mira's eyes widen.

"Yeah," I say. "My mom used to live in Gold River. Grew up here. And one day, she was kidnapped by the Grand Dame and used as a sacrifice for their ritual. But the ritual didn't work. It backfired. It killed everyone in the hotel, except for my mother. My mom got out. She ran as far away as she could. Down to Florida, where she grew up and had a kid. But she was always a little . . . haunted. She had nightmares about this place. Most kids grow up with fairy tales or nursery rhymes. I grew up with stories about the Carlisle Hotel. And when she died, I knew that the Carlisle held the answer.

"So I researched everything I could. At first, I'd thought it was all made up. But the more I dug, the more I discovered. Not only about the hotel, but about the truth of where and why it was built. The truth of the people who built it, the Society that funded it. All led by the Grand Dame. All in the name of finding immortality. So I reached out to people, others who were in the Society, and pretended to be a member.

It's *amazing* what you can learn from people online. And once you start with one little lie, all the others become easier.

"I learned how the ritual was done, and where, and when. And so, I packed everything and came here, alone, and I registered at school, and I waited. Until the Dare. Until the planets aligned. Until the perfect moment. Until tonight."

"But, no—your dad—"

"Is back in Florida. He never would have come back here. I've been squatting in that old house the entire time. Why else do you think I never invited you over?"

There's so much shock and betrayal in Mira's eyes that I almost laugh again.

"You lied," she says. "You lied about everything."

"Not everything," I say, grinning. "I *am* from Florida. And I *was* made fun of. The things those kids said . . . You can imagine, then, how excited I was to learn that one of the things needed to restart the ritual was fear. We needed everyone in the hotel to be afraid. To raise the energy needed to bring back the ghosts and fully enliven the Grand Dame."

"And you did such a good job with that, my dear," the

Grand Dame says, smiling. Rohan struggles against her, but he gets nowhere. *"They were so convinced. Their fear tasted delicious."*

I smile. It's nice to feel praised for a job well done.

"How could you?" Mira asks. "How could you do this to us? How could you *trust* her? She tried to hurt your mom!"

"And she's the only way to get my mom back," I say sharply. I look at her. Despite the flush of victory, there are tears in my eyes. "My mom was the only one who really knew me. Who really loved and cared about me. When she died . . . when she died, my entire world fell apart. The Grand Dame can reach across the veil between the living and dead to bring her back." My resolve falters slightly. "I'll do anything to get her back."

"But why me?" Mira asks. "I thought we were friends."

The betrayal in her words is a stab to my heart, but I push it away. I had to do this. I *had* to.

"I wasn't certain at first," I say. "I just knew the ritual needed someone pure and selfless to be completed, and when I met you, I couldn't imagine it being anyone else. And when I learned you'd been having visions, too, that you'd been pulled to this place, well . . . I figured you had to be it."

"*I was impressed by how sensitive she was,*" the Grand Dame says. "*You, Jasmine, have always been in tune to this place, thanks to your mother's ties. But Mira here . . . her qualities called to me like a bell. The hotel knew she was the one to complete the ritual, and I was ever so grateful for your help in bringing her here. Now, the time draws near. We must begin.*"

I nod. The ghosts holding Mira bring her over to the Grand Dame. She releases Rohan, who is in turn snatched by another ghost, who drags him, kicking and fighting, to the corner.

"It will never work!" Rohan says. "It failed before."

"You're wrong," I say. "I've done my research. Tonight, it will work perfectly. You made sure of that."

Instantly, his resistance stops. He stands, limp and scared, and stares at me.

"The ritual failed the first time because it needed a *willing* sacrifice. And you just ensured we had one."

His eyes widen. "What?"

"Mira offered to sacrifice herself to save you," I

say. "So, in a way, this is your fault, too. After all, we never would have come here if not for you."

I smile wide. Then, as he starts to struggle again, I turn to the Grand Dame, who has both hands on Mira's shoulders.

"Do it," I say. "Bring my mom back."

"As we swore, so shall it be. A willing sacrifice for your mother."

"I'm not willing anymore!" Mira says. "I take it back. I don't want to be a sacrifice."

"Silence!" the Grand Dame says. A pulse of magic, and Mira's jaw snaps shut. *"You already swore. And your word, I'm afraid, is bond. Shall we begin?"*

I nod. Begin to chant the words my mother sang as a nursery rhyme.

I visualize her as the ghosts pick up the chant,
as the Grand Dame summons the power,
as the ritual resumes.

In my dreams, the door leading here led to death. It always led to death.

I just never said that it was mine.

37

Light flashes around Mira, a brilliant green, and the symbols flaring on the walls twist and twine. Serpentine spirals of light stretch between Mira and the Grand Dame.

As Mira fades.

As Mira becomes a permanent resident of the hotel.

As the Grand Dame glows with immortal life.

But that isn't the only magic happening in the room.

The symbols behind the Grand Dame merge. They twist and arc into a doorway, a doorway filled with heavy blackness and glimmering stars.

A shape appears in the doorway, pulled forward by the Grand Dame's powers.

Pulled forward by her promise. And mine.

When the shadowy figure steps outside the portal, relief floods me. I rush forward, into the warm, inviting arms of my mother.

Tears flood from my eyes. Mom wraps her arms tight around me, holding me close. I bury my head against her chest, sobbing so hard I can't hear the chanting in the room. All I hear is her own crying. All I feel is her warmth.

She's back.

She's back.

Suddenly, the last memories I have of her—her wasting away in the hospital bed of a sickness no doctor could place, a disease that I *knew* stemmed from here—vanish. All I can think while wrapped in her embrace are the good memories: cuddling up and eating pizza together, singing off-key to music in the car, dancing in the kitchen while making dinner. She's back. My mom is back from the dead.

It was worth it.

It was all worth it.

"Jasmine," she whispers. "I missed you so much."

"I did, too, Momma." I sniff, and a fresh wave of tears comes over me. "I told you I'd make you healthy again," I say, remembering the final words I whispered to her in the hospital. "I promised."

"And you kept that promise," she replies, then pauses. "But how did we end up here?"

I blink and look around.

We're no longer in the basement.

Instead, we're in a hotel room.

The door is open, and I can see the number—333—on the gold plate. Warm light glows in the hall, and when I look around, I realize the room is set up perfectly—no dust, no sign of age. The two queen beds are freshly made and even have mints on the pillows. There's a tea set with a steaming kettle on the dresser. There are even fresh flowers on the nightstand.

Mira and Rohan and the Grand Dame are nowhere to be seen.

Until . . .

A shadow falls over the doorway, and moments later the Grand Dame sweeps in. She no longer looks monstrous. Instead, she is human and utterly gorgeous, a smile on her lips.

"You," my mom hisses.

The Grand Dame just smiles wider.

"I would hope," she says, *"that since I have given you back your life, you will forgive me for that one minor incident all those years ago? The past is the past, after all."*

My mother swallows hard.

"I don't expect thanks, of course," the Grand Dame continues. *"That should all go to your daughter."*

"What?" my mom asks. She stands up, and I feel my bubble of happiness slipping away. "What do you mean?"

"Why, she is the one who helped me complete my ritual. She granted me immortality. And in exchange, I brought you back from the dead. An even trade, I believe."

Now, when my mother looks at me, it's not love and relief that I see in her eyes, but fear.

A fear of me.

"What did you do?" my mother asks.

"What I had to," I reply. "I did it for you. So we could be together again."

The Grand Dame chuckles and turns from the

room. But she pauses outside the door, her immaculate nails resting on the doorframe.

"I'll leave you two to talk," she says. *"You have so much to catch up on, and forever to do it."*

She leaves, and my mom only stares at me.

And for the first time since I put this plan into action, I start to wonder if it was truly worth it.

Epilogue

In my dreams, I wander down the long hallway.
Pulled toward a door that doesn't spell the end, but
a beginning.

In my waking life, too, I wander the halls of the
Carlisle Hotel. Only now, the hotel is bustling with
life. A half-life, at least.

I smile and nod at the elderly gentleman and his
granddaughter as they walk past me, heading to dinner. Neither of them quite dead, but not fully alive,
either. So long as they stay here in the hotel, though,
they get to exist. All because of my help.

They treat me like royalty.

"Miss Jasmine," the older man says. "Miss Sarah."

My mother smiles and nods at him as we pass.

Music drifts through the halls. Music and laughter and life. So much life.

I squeeze my mother's hand as we walk the other direction. Toward our shared room. Room 333. The only room that had been vacant. Until now.

Something catches my eye as we near the room. I pause.

"You go and get ready," I tell my mom. "I'll be right in."

She smiles at me, but there isn't the same warmth and love as before. She hasn't said much since I brought her back, but that's okay. She'll forgive me soon. She'll understand. Eventually.

She's back. That's all that's important.

She glides down the hall, and I turn my attention back to the window.

Outside, snow drifts down. I can see the lights of Gold River beyond.

The Grand Dame is out there, somewhere. No doubt gathering more guests for the hungry Carlisle Hotel. Unlike the rest of us, she can leave here.

I should have been more specific when I asked

her to bring my mom back. She did. Of course she did—she swore it when she first spoke to me in the fire in the lobby, and her word was her bond. A word is always a bond.

But she didn't say she would let my mom and me *leave*.

We're stuck here.

Forever.

Just like the other guests.

At least we're here together.

I press my hand to the windowpane.

"I don't expect you to understand," I say.

In reflection, Mira and Bradley stare back. They're stuck here, too, in some sort of other-world. A limbo. I don't often see them. I don't think they like seeing me. The true me.

Granted, Bradley saw the true me. He saw it the moment I let go of his hand and let him fall back into the swimming pool.

Rohan is somewhere back in town. He's the only one who got out, because of Mira's deal. No doubt he's still trying to convince the mayor to burn down the hotel or something ludicrous. It will never work.

Now that the Grand Dame is back, the town is under her thumb once more.

Mira steps forward. Pounds her fists on the windowpane.

It doesn't make a sound.

"I had to do it," I say. "For her. I love her so much."

Mira yells something. It's probably for the best that I don't hear what she screams.

Down the hall, the bells chime for dinner.

I reach over and pull the curtain on the window, blocking Mira and Bradley from sight.

Eventually, they'll come around. They'll forgive me, just like my mom will. They'll all forgive me, and everything will go back to the way it was: my mom loving me, and my friends trusting me. Maybe the Grand Dame will even let Mira out. We'll all be happy again.

We have to be.

We have an eternity together, after all.

Acknowledgments

To say that 2020 and 2021 have been difficult years would be an understatement. It wasn't always possible to find a light in the dark times, but oddly enough, writing creepy stories helped get me through. For that, I am grateful, and I hope this and other books have helped you escape the harsher reality, even if only for a little while.

As always, this book wouldn't have been possible without the overwhelming support of Scholastic and my amazing team. I am so grateful to you all, but wish to give a special thanks to David Levithan, for his editorial brilliance, and to Jana Haussmann, for being my number-one cheerleader. These books have been life-changing, for me and so many readers, and I owe it all to your combined genius.

My thanks, of course, to my parents. To my father, for getting me skiing from age four and exposing me to the perfect backdrop for this wintry mountainside tale. To my mother, for always supporting my writing endeavors. And my brother, for being the embodiment of perseverance.

But most of all, I want to thank you, dear reader. These books wouldn't have been possible if there hadn't been an eager audience awaiting them. I'm so grateful for your continued support and voracious appetite for words—and I'm *especially* grateful to those of you who took the time to write me! Your letters and drawings never fail to make my day.

I hope I can keep scaring you for years to come.

About the Author

K. R. Alexander is the pseudonym for author Alex R. Kahler.

As K. R., he writes creepy middle grade books for brave young readers. As Alex—his actual first name—he writes fantasy novels for adults and teens. In both cases, he loves writing fiction drawn from true life experiences. (But this book can't be real . . . can it?) Alex has traveled the world collecting strange and fascinating tales, from the misty moors of Scotland to the humid jungles of Hawaii. He is always on the move, as he believes there is much more to life than what meets the eye.

You can learn more about his travels and books, including *The Collector, The Collected, The Undrowned, The Fear Zone,* and the books in the Scare Me series, on his website cursedlibrary.com. He looks forward to scaring you again . . . soon.

Read more from

K. R. Alexander...

if you dare

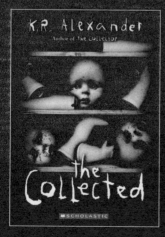

Be afraid.
Be very, very afraid...

SCHOLASTIC
scholastic.com

ALEXANDER-SCAREME